FOR LOVE
AND HONOR

FOR LOVE
AND HONOR

•

MARILYN STORIE

AVALON BOOKS
THOMAS BOUREGY AND COMPANY, INC.
401 LAFAYETTE STREET
NEW YORK, NEW YORK 10003

© Copyright 1998 by Marilyn Storie
Library of Congress Catalog Card Number 98-96225
ISBN 0-8034-9303-7

PRINTED IN THE UNITED STATES OF AMERICA
ON ACID-FREE PAPER
BY HADDON CRAFTSMEN, BLOOMSBURG, PENNSYLVANIA

Dedicated to my family

Chapter One

*H*is *burning eyes met her startled blue ones and
Sarah felt her resolve weakening. A lowly governess
paid the beggarly sum of six pounds a year . . . who
was she to deny Sir Randolph Heaston anything he
wanted? As if he sensed her uncertainty, his strong
arms reached out to cage her again, encircling her so
tightly this time that she gasped with alarm.*

*"Sir Randolph . . . no," Sarah stammered. But the
lord of Greystones was not listening. His raven locks
brushed against her cheeks as he bent to kiss the stone
white hollow of her neck. She shivered, feeling the
press of his lips as a further torture to her senses. His
hands crept expertly through her wheat-colored hair,
removing the tortoiseshell pin that held her tresses*

primly in place. Sarah froze as he forced her modest neckline down to immodest depths and planted a burning kiss on her quivering neck. Breathing hoarsely, he picked her up easily and strode to the curtained bed. Casting its velvet draperies aside, he set Sarah down as carefully as if she were a china ornament and liable to break.

Defiantly, Sarah sat up. She drew her neckline back up to its proper place and shook a wayward curl out of her angry eyes. ''I may be your servant, sir—but before God I swear that I will not be your mistress!''

Jenny Lane set down her pen and smiled impishly. Sarah was turning out even better than Priscilla Kensington, the orphaned street waif she had given life in *The King's Inn.* Priscilla had been fun, Jenny thought, but Sarah was better—Sarah had spunk. Jenny glanced absently at the clock and started. It was almost six o'clock and she still had to dress for dinner. If she didn't hurry, she'd be late for the third night in a row.

Jenny sighed and reluctantly pulled herself from a world she sometimes found easier to put on than a comfortable dress. She slipped nimbly out of her stonewashed jeans and purple sweatshirt.

Her toes tingled as she walked across the cold marble of the bathroom floor. Wondering what she should wear, she glanced into the adjoining dressing room. Her gaze fell on the wheat-colored carpet and a smile touched her bow-shaped lips. It was the color of the carpet that had given her the idea for Sarah's hair. She was becoming an expert at spinning straw into gold, she thought, suddenly glum. Clad only in a wispy bra and panties, she turned to stare into the bathroom mirror, cocking her head at the sight of her own expertly cut mane.

It was so black it was really blue-black: the color of ripe blackberries. The thick hair was held back from her forehead with a cheerful plaid band, revealing Jenny's expressive almond-shaped eyes. Her hair was in vivid contrast to her translucent ivory skin. Such a coveted complexion—as her great-grandmother was fond of telling her—was rarely seen these days. Blood would tell, the Old One would always add imperiously. Jenny squirmed with embarrassment, remembering how all of the family within earshot would nod in polite agreement.

She took a washcloth and scrubbed furiously at her perfect face. She tilted the sides of the three-pane mirror forward—a childhood trick. Generations of coddled ancestors popped into view to stare back at her. She made a face, glaring with dissatisfaction at their delicately arched noses and high cheekbones. *Why can't I just be what I want to be?* Jenny wondered. Twenty-two and—

The familiar double click of canes crossing the marble sounded, and Jenny grabbed hastily for her rose-colored bathrobe.

"Just a moment, Great-grandmother."

The Old One, as Jenny's great-grandmother preferred to be called, did not insist on this tribute from her. Jenny knew it was because she was the older woman's favorite. As the oldest living member of the household, she insisted on exacting that form of address from all others.

"It's too late—I saw you," the Old One declared with satisfaction. "You look as graceful as a willow."

Coloring, Jenny thrust her arms into the bathrobe and pulled it tight. She caught sight of the Old One tilting dangerously forward on her ebony canes, and she rushed back from the dressing room to help her. "Sit here, Great-grandmother."

"Don't fuss. I'm perfectly all right."

"You know you're going to fall." Jenny firmly lowered the tiny woman into a wicker armchair and took her canes. The tall canes were really staffs. Carved with swirling flowers and embedded with miniature ivory petals, they had been passed down from generation to generation. Jenny padded barefoot across the pink marble to prop them against the wall and turned back to the Old One.

Her great-grandmother was looking down at her own feet. Jenny's heart stirred with pity. Encased in satin slippers, they were ludicrously tiny and misshapen—the bane of her great-grandmother's life. She watched as the Old One's expression changed from its habitual tight circle of satisfaction into a grimace of pain.

"A cushion, please," she told Jenny. "It's these wretched feet of mine acting up again. Every time I change position, something else seems to hurt. Now my back is aching."

Jenny dubiously studied the ramrod-straight back. *I've never once seen her slouch,* she thought. She darted in and propped a tasseled cushion behind the old woman's back so she could sit comfortably. "Is that better?"

"Yes. A good thing you'll never need these dratted canes. I want them buried with me." Her eyes blazed suddenly. "Or maybe I'll have them burned."

"You should give them to a museum."

"Hah! No museum would have them." She looked sharply at Jenny. "Now stop mooning about and put on something pretty. Edward Li is coming to dinner."

"Oh, Great-grandmother." Jenny's face fell. "He's such a weird guy."

"He's not—he's a perfectly respectable businessman and you should be honored he's willing to marry a girl like you."

Jenny knew what she meant. With the exception of her younger brother Ben, with whom she literally saw eye-to-eye, Jenny was unlike the rest of the Lanes. She was five feet nine inches tall. To her much shorter family, it was a remarkable height, overshadowing even Jenny's slim beauty. When the Lanes had first come to this harbor city ten years ago, there had been no sign that she and Ben would grow so tall. The Old One, she knew, was convinced it was something in the drinking water. Her own husband, a white missionary in Hong Kong, had been as short as the Chinese people he ministered to daily.

"I'm perfectly comfortable with the way I am," Jenny said now, and stalked to her dressing room. "If Edward doesn't like it, then it's his problem."

I'd never get away with saying that if we still lived in Hong Kong, Jenny thought. The Lanes had been among the first of the big merchant families to take flight before the rights to Hong Kong reverted to mainland China. It struck her as ironic that the Old One— grown sensitive over a lifetime of political upheaval to any new threat of change—was the one who had insisted on moving. She had given Jenny's father no peace until he had agreed to leave.

Jenny was glad they had moved to Vancouver. Things were more relaxed in the Canadian city, but many things reminded her of her childhood home. Like Hong Kong, Vancouver was first and foremost a harbor city, as picturesque as only a city next to the Pacific Ocean could be. It wasn't as warm—Hong Kong had been subtropical—but it had a rainy season of sorts, and certainly no one missed the absence of typhoons. *And it's not so crowded here,* Jenny thought as she studied the dresses in her closet. *There's more room and fewer people.* She loved the look of the lawns flowing like green velvet over the rich delta soil. Seemingly endless crops sprang up without any apparent need for replenishment.

The family, too, had taken root and thrived. It was an exciting city, bursting with new growth and new ideas. Jenny thought of her brother's preference for outrageously baggy clothes, and her own daytime uniform of blue jeans and sweatshirts, and frowned briefly. No, she could never live like that in Hong Kong.

Jenny returned from her rummage through the walk-in closet with a see-through dress that would leave nothing to the imagination. Her great-grandmother was half dozing in the warm evening sunshine. She sleepily raised her iron gray head. Jenny held out the dress, somewhat wickedly, for her to inspect.

"Oh my," the Old One said, shocked from her reverie into speaking English. "Do women dress like that?"

"It's okay, Great-grandmother." Jenny revealed the beige slip dress she had kept hidden behind her back. "This goes with it."

"In that case, I suppose . . . but are you sure?" her great-grandmother asked doubtfully.

"It's the perfect thing for a hot summer's night." Jenny's voice was reassuring, but her eyes were dancing.

Jenny loved her. But she couldn't help it—she loved to tease her. In many ways, the Old One was the most progressive of all the family, Jenny thought. But in other ways, her great-grandmother was a rock of stubbornness. She insisted on good manners and respect for tradition. She had drilled both into Jenny for many years.

Jenny smiled, remembering her earliest childhood memory. In it, she struggled to take the few steps that would bring her into her great-grandmother's arms. She remembered looking up with drooling love at the wrinkled face. *I still love her,* Jenny thought. *But I wish she'd stop treating me like a child.*

Jenny thought of tormenting her further. She had a pair of spectacularly garish earrings that she had purchased for a Halloween party two years ago. The sequined balls dangled almost to her shoulders. She darted a quick glance at her beloved great-grandmother and surprised a look of patient suffering on her face.

"I'll be ready soon," she said, relenting.

Jenny retreated to the dressing room and quickly put on the cotton underdress. Her fingers flew up the rows of tiny mother-of-pearl buttons. She slipped the transparent voile dress over her head. She straightened it, and the gauzy layers drifted with easy grace to within an inch of the floor, emphasizing every inch of her height.

It should upset Edward, Jenny thought delightedly. After all, he was only five feet six inches tall. To double the impact, Jenny searched in her closet for her highest platform shoes. She found them at last, a pair of strappy leather sandals that added another three inches to her height.

The Old One gave her a sidelong look when she returned, but said nothing. "Do your feet give you pain, Great-grandmother?" Jenny asked hastily. She helped her tiny great-grandmother, who weighed no more than eighty pounds, to rise to her feet.

"Not tonight, child . . . tonight I could walk for miles if I thought you would look on Edward Li with favor."

Jenny smiled politely and looked away. How could she tell her that Edward Li was the last man she wanted to marry? He was successful, always immaculately groomed, and ten years older than Jenny. Her family had pronounced it a perfect match.

But Jenny knew what her future would be. A woman of her family did not work outside the home. She was her husband's helpmate and raised his children. End of story, Jenny thought. She wanted more than that from life. *There has to be more than that,* she thought desperately. Her own family barely tolerated her "scribbling." Would Edward allow her to continue after they were married? She somehow doubted he would approve of the way she lost track of time, no matter how well her books sold.

Jenny wished she could be more like her mother. She was a perfect role model—and maybe that was why she had failed to inspire Jenny to be like her. Next to her mother, Jenny felt imperfect. A leading light of Vancouver's arts society, her impeccably groomed mother floated from one fund-raising affair to the next. Still beautiful at forty-three, she was the perfect hostess to her husband's ever-growing circle of business acquaintances. She was content with that and seeing to her children's welfare.

But it was one thing to support the arts and quite another to be creative yourself, Jenny had discovered. Writing about love, the search for love, the meaning of love, the discovery of that one special person to spend the rest of your days with . . . it had given her a decidedly different goal. And if she had learned anything, she thought, it was that settling for anything but the real thing was the biggest mistake a woman could make.

She guided the Old One carefully around the mahogany bench that jutted out at the end of the upstairs hall. Jenny took her canes at the top of the stairs, fidgeting as she waited for her great-grandmother to doggedly make her way down the stairs. The Old One gripped the polished banister, lowering herself carefully from step to step. Her great-grandmother had steadfastly refused to let the family install an electric lift for the stairs.

"When the day comes that I can no longer move myself around, I'll stay in bed," she had often told Jenny.

By the time they reached the formal dining room, everyone was seating themselves at the dining table. Edward was chatting with her father, his confident tone at odds with his nervously tapping foot. Her fiancé's suit jacket bulged importantly, as always, she saw—she wondered if he'd bring his mobile phone to the wedding.

Edward fell silent when he caught sight of her. Jenny averted her face and led her great-grandmother to the head of the table. The Old One eyed the comfortably upholstered chair and moved faster, reminding Jenny of a marathon athlete catching sight of the finish line. She let go of Jenny's arm and uttered a groan of relief as she sank into the chair.

Jenny was determined not to make eye contact with Edward. Instead, she gazed about the room as if she had never seen it before. She studied the high arches of the spacious windows. Her eyes drifted over the sea green brocade of the drapes that descended in stiff folds. They had been artfully pressed to resemble an open fan. The antique rosewood sideboard gleamed with the richness of much-polished wood, and the floral centerpiece of tiger lilies and miniature yellow roses was reflected in the high gloss of the lacquered mahogany table. The crystal chandelier sparkled dimly overhead.

Jenny glumly put her damask napkin on her lap and hoped the meal would pass swiftly. *Maybe I'll get time to finish another chapter,* she thought. She felt her mother's eyes on her and started.

Her mother wore a trim Alfred Sung suit that made her look the most efficient of hostesses. ''Jenny, you look lovely.'' Her voice ended on a questioning note.

Yes, Jenny thought with satisfaction. *I also look tall.*

Mrs. Lane next twisted her head to smile brightly at Edward. ''Edward,'' she said archly, ''doesn't Jenny look pretty tonight?''

''Like a pear blossom drifting on moonlight,'' Edward said politely.

Jenny looked up, scarcely daring to breathe. *Why, that was almost poetry.* Startled, Jenny wondered briefly if she had been wrong about him. She raised her head. But Edward's eyes were less polite, and her heart shrank as she tried to meet his gaze. Their obsidian centers studied Jenny hungrily, seeking to pierce the deceptively transparent dress. Jenny reddened and stared down at her lap.

How dare he look at me like that? she thought, enraged. But with a sinking heart, Jenny remembered that he had every reason to examine the woman he was going to marry. And every right, she realized still more dismally.

Jenny's brother gave her a sympathetic glance. He knew how she felt about Edward. Alike in more than height, the two were as modern in their tastes and outlook as the rest of the family was old-fashioned. Ben's knuckles were rapping softly, but insistently, on the table. He was keeping time to an unheard melody, Jenny knew. It was probably a new one that he was trying to work out in his head. Their mother arched her eyebrows warningly and he stopped, his cheerful face suddenly embarrassed.

"Did you have a busy day at the warehouse?" Jenny asked him quickly.

"The same old same old," Ben replied gratefully. "Life in the cracks." He ran his hand through his conservatively cut black hair—how ironic, Jenny thought, that the family didn't realize the cut was back in style—and gave her a conspiratorial wink. He knew better than to ask her how the book was going in front of the family.

Ben worked hard at the warehouse during the day, exhibiting an acceptable ability to match the right goods with the right customer. But at night he played rock music with a band, secretly dreaming of becoming a professional musician one day. His hands were made to hold a guitar, just as Jenny's own slender fingers were unable to get through the day without expressing her thoughts on paper. He had told his dreams only to her, and she had likewise confided in him.

Jenny loved her brother, but she couldn't help feeling a stab of envy. At twenty, Ben was a man, and that made all the difference. She watched her brother's artistically long fingers raise a goblet of water to his mouth before they returned to tapping, this time discreetly hidden under the table. The rest of the family considered her writing a childish hobby that she would soon outgrow. But no matter what they thought, it was something she was proud of, she told herself defiantly. And in an odd sort of way, she supposed her success was due to them—they had never let her do anything else. She had sold two books, but no one except Ben seemed to appreciate her success in the heady world of historical romance. Now their friendship, too, was to be put away—like a toy outgrown by children. She would soon no longer be able to share the secrets of her heart with her brother.

Sheng brought sharks' fin soup to the table, and Jenny immediately knew that her mother had spared no expense to impress their guest. She made a face of distaste. The cost was ridiculous—at least seventy dollars a bowl—and she was always horrified at the thought of the poor sharks losing their fins. She glared at the serving man, and he glared back, automatically bypassing her.

"The costs of shipping are rising," Edward remarked conversationally to her father. He stared impassively at the steaming bowl Sheng set in front of him. "What are you doing to manage?"

What a creep, Jenny thought. *I bet he eats it.*

"We do everything we can to keep our costs down," her father said, looking alert at the prospect of discussing business. "But our bottom line keeps rising, thanks to the change in fuel prices."

"Have you considered shipping by air?" Edward nibbled delicately at a roll, his snub nose wrinkling and reminding Jenny of a rabbit's. "There are some goods that are light enough to be cost-effective."

"Not nowadays," Sidney Lane said, his smooth forehead wrinkling as he considered the suggestion. "There's such a monopoly that it's difficult to find anyone willing to undercut prices by much more than the regular rate unless you do all your business with them."

Despite his worries over shipping costs, her father's decision to concentrate on expanding markets for goods from the Far East had been a good one, Jenny knew. More Hong Kong Chinese were arriving in Vancouver daily. And with mainland China eager to continue strengthening trade with the West, the Lane business was growing by leaps and bounds throughout the Pacific Rim.

While the two men talked, earnestly dissecting the pros and cons of freighting by air, Jenny stared covertly at her fiancé. He looked like what he was: a successful accountant. In a subdued way, he was attractive enough, she supposed. But the unrelieved thin line of his lips, the stiff way in which he held himself, and the habit he had of prissily clearing his throat from time to time with a hand held to his mouth . . . she had no more wish to marry him than she did to stop writing. *With only two months to go before the wedding, I don't have the luxury of pretending it isn't going to happen anymore,* she thought suddenly.

Jenny suffered in silence—sulking, her mother called it—throughout the six-course meal, barely touching even the most extravagant course. The Kobe beef, shipped from Tokyo by way of Hong Kong, was sliced so thinly it was almost as translucent as Jenny's dress. Even Ben, who could ordinarily care less about food, moaned with enjoyment at the taste of the fragile slices melting in his mouth.

Edward, seated directly across from her, kept trying to catch her eye, and failing that, he glared at his plate. To Jenny's disgust, he accepted a second bowl of soup. The dinner dragged on slowly. Her mother smiled brilliantly from time to time, asking after Edward's family and urging more of the succulent beef on him. Jenny toyed grimly with the salad Sheng had grudgingly brought her. Dessert proved to be three kinds of fresh melon carved into neat pyramids. Sheng returned once more with a silver tureen and uncovered it to display candied plums and apricots.

Tea was finally brought in, signaling the end of the meal. Jenny, as the daughter of the house, rose politely to serve it. First—she hesitated—to Edward.

He caught her hand in his as she offered him the fragile cup, holding her trembling fingers longer than necessary. Edward's hand was plump and unmuscled. It felt like a garden slug. She pulled back instinctively, and the cup crashed to the table, shattering with a tinkle and splashing tea onto the front of her dress.

"I'm so sorry." Jenny gasped. "Excuse my clumsiness." Edward looked up angrily, his eyes flaring at the insult. But they quickly narrowed in interest when he spotted the clinging front of Jenny's wet dress.

"I must change," she said, embarrassed and then angry when she saw where his eyes were fixed. "Excuse my clumsiness," she repeated, coldly bowing. She backed awkwardly from the room. Ben opened his mouth as if he meant to laugh, and then, looking quickly at the rest of the family, he shut it abruptly. Her parents and great-grandmother, rigid with shock, stared at her. Jenny fled.

Up in her room, Jenny changed into a new dress— she first held it up to the light to ensure it was *not* transparent—and sat down on the edge of her bed. Her gaze moved wistfully over the stuffed dolls and lighted on the giant dollhouse her father had bought her when she was twelve. She had protested she was too big for such a toy and asked for a spy kit instead. Jenny glared at the Victorian replica. Its living spaces were laid out as rigidly as those of a beehive. As usual, her family's notion of what was best for her had won out.

She looked resentfully at the portraits of relatives above her bed. They stared down on Jenny from their secure niches in the walls, smiling wordlessly. Had they all allowed their lives to be arranged for them? Jenny wondered if even one of them had ever dared to take a chance.

She leaned against the window, relishing the coolness of the glass against her hot cheek. Pale moths were swooping at the window, attracted to the bright glow from the room. She drew back in distaste, repulsed by the soft thump of their bodies against the invisible glass. She thought of Edward waiting for her below and shuddered.

Jenny fetched her manuscript and sat back down on the bed. She fanned the pages out on the down quilt and stared at them. What a difference there was between her life and the one she had planned for Sarah! She thought of her heroine, wild and defiant in the face of Lord Randolph's unwanted attentions. Sarah would give in eventually, she knew. But not until she was satisfied that Lord Randolph was in love with her. And that she was in love with him, Jenny thought. That was something that Sarah, poor as she was, would insist on before giving herself to any man. Jenny's heart gave an uncomfortable leap. Why, that was exactly how she felt. She could never marry a man she didn't love.

Jenny straightened. It was no use pretending things were other than they were. Unless she took some responsibility for her own life—and quickly—it was going to be over. She sat motionless for a long moment. And then she rose. She pulled open a drawer of the bureau. It slid out easily. She stared down at the neatly folded clothes for another long moment. She thought again of Edward, and her face suddenly cleared.

She got her carry-all bag from the closet and began packing. She really only needed jeans and sweatshirts. But what would she do for money? She had little cash. Her credit card could be used, she decided, but quickly—before the family realized she was missing. After packing her clothes and toiletries, she grabbed her purse and snatched up the manuscript, stuffing them both into the bag. She zipped it shut and shot a furtive look at the portraits above her. One faded great-aunt, thin-lipped and stern, looked decidedly disapproving, she decided. The great-aunt's hair was pulled back into controlled waves with a decorative comb. She looked a lot like Jenny's mother. Jenny lifted her hands dreamily to her own hair, coaxing it into disarray.

Holding the navy canvas bag tightly against her side, Jenny walked quietly down the stairs and tiptoed to the foyer. Her heart was beating with excitement. Feeling exactly like one of her heroines, she inched slowly around the corner and moved to the back entrance used by the servants. Her hand froze when the dead-bolt lock clicked open with a loud snap. Hesitating, she was relieved to note that the murmur of conversation from the dining room was continuing unchecked.

Taking a deep breath, Jenny scooted out the door. She fled down the brick walkway and into the night. Remembering Dorothy in *The Wizard of Oz*, Jenny smiled down at the bricks. Where would her brick road lead her? With growing satisfaction, Jenny realized that she didn't know.

She looked up, savoring her first moments of freedom. The sky was studded with limitless stars, and each one loomed like a possibility to Jenny. For the first time in her life she would learn what it was like to make her own choices—her own decisions.

She crept to the front of the house and stared, struck by how unfamiliar everything looked. Had she really grown up here? All of the houses on the winding curve of Marine Drive, including her own, looked strange and unfamiliar in the orange glow of the streetlights.

She could see her family and Edward through the silken sheers hung across the dining-room window. A practiced laugh rang out—her mother's. Jenny thought cynically of the polite chatter she herself had confidently pronounced at the tea parties she had once hosted for her dolls.

Jenny took a deep breath of the clear night air, appreciative of its crisp ocean scent. She remembered the story her father had told her: that the ocean breeze was an old woman who came with her broom to clean the air. He had never failed to tuck her into bed every night, she remembered.

What's the matter with me? Jenny thought. *This is no time to hesitate.* She shook her head from side to side, imagining that she was ridding it of the cobwebs of childhood. She shouldn't be thinking of the past, she told herself. It was time to think of the future.

She walked swiftly past the curtained windows and circled the dark rhododendron bushes lining the lawn. She darted out onto the sidewalk so quickly that she stubbed a toe. Jenny began running past the perfectly groomed lawns of Marine Drive and then—fearful that a neighbor would see her and ask her why she was running—she slowed to what she believed was a brisk walk. She was unaware that if anyone had seen her, they would have described her gait as flying.

Jenny plunged forward eagerly, beckoned by the insistent pull of the city lights shining below.

What was out there in this vast world that her family was so determined to keep from her? She vowed that she would find out.

Chapter Two

A yawning crack in the wall struggled from one end to the other above the dusty drapes. *It's the shape of a rainbow,* Jenny thought, unperturbed by what it suggested of the foundation below. Instead, it struck her as a favorable omen. The apartment was small—scarcely larger than her bathroom at home. Still, as the landlady had said, it was furnished: with an ancient tweed couch that folded out into a bed, a steel kitchen table accompanied by mismatched chairs and—Jenny was elated to see—an oak desk scarred with kicks and cigarette burns.

She looked curiously out the window. The old building was in the heart of Chinatown. The crowds she saw below on the wide cement pavements were mostly families. Nearly everyone carried parcels and string-net shopping bags. She studied the people with pleased interest.

''The rent's two hundred a week,'' the landlady said in Cantonese. ''Plus one hundred deposit.'' She was a dry bone of a woman, thin with age and disappointment. She wore a cotton housedress, formerly blue, but washed so many times it was now a dispirited gray.

Jenny paid her eagerly and accepted the tarnished key. ''No smoking, no pets, no loud music,'' the landlady reeled off. She cackled suddenly, exposing a pair of ill-fitting dentures. ''Anything else is up to you.'' She turned to leave. ''Garbage pickup's on Tuesday,'' she called back over her shoulder. The door shut.

Free! Jenny spread her arms wide and spun three times across the orange shag carpet, fetching up a nose's length from the wall.

Withdrawing nothing but her own money—a move she did not dare repeat for fear her family would be alerted—had given her a first taste of just how delicious independence could be. But to have her own place! The weekly rent was less than she ordinarily spent on a dress. She should be able to manage just fine until the book was finished.

Three days later, she was pleased to discover herself at the halfway point of the book. *Won't Lynn be happy,* she thought. Jenny pulled the black rotary phone to her—*what an antique,* she marveled—and clumsily dialed her agent's number.

"They liked the first three chapters," Lynn Jennings said. Jenny could sense her excitement over the phone. She pictured the tiny woman, feet up, in her paper-stacked office. "Considering how well *The King's Inn* did, I think we'll be able to manage a hefty press run, too."

"That's great, Lynn. I'm glad they like it. Um . . . what kind of an advance are they offering?"

"The usual . . . but Jenny—"

"What?"

"They want the whole book completed before they'll fork over the money this time."

"Oh, Lynn . . ."

"Come on, Jenny—you know you took forever to finish *The King's Inn.* They had to change the print date twice, and that's not exactly the way to a publisher's heart."

Things were different then, Jenny wanted to say. She hadn't worked as hard as she could have because she didn't need the money before. But now she did, Jenny realized uneasily. For a moment she thought of explaining her situation to Lynn. She was one of the best agents in the business . . . brightly efficient and absolutely unforgiving when it came to deadlines.

It suddenly dawned on Jenny that the change in her

circumstances would make no difference to Lynn. How did that expression go? If she wanted to talk the talk, then she would have to walk the walk. For the first time in her life there was no one to bail her out but herself.

"Lynn?" Jenny ventured. "I'll get it to you in eight weeks."

"Do you mean that?" Lynn's voice crackled with enthusiasm. Jenny heard a thump, and she knew that Lynn's feet had jumped from her desk and hit the floor.

"I do." She was almost finished with the fifth chapter, and eight weeks would be enough if she stuck to it. It would have to be.

"Great . . . and Jenny?"

"Yes?"

"The reading editor wants you to warm it up a bit. You know . . . put in some real love scenes for a change."

Jenny was nonplussed. "Gosh, Lynn. I thought that's what I was doing." A blush that began somewhere in the region of her toes shot up to her face.

"It's not me, honey," Lynn added hastily. "I *love* your stuff. Nobody does historic romances better. But the editor said she wants realistic love scenes, so throw in a bit of spice to keep her happy. Okay?"

"Okay," Jenny said dully. She said good-bye and hung up the phone. Pushing the pages aside, she got up from the desk. She flung herself on the couch and then shifted grudgingly to avoid the stab of a broken spring.

It had never occurred to her that her love scenes might not seem real. What did Lynn expect her to do? Go out and have an affair? Jenny blushed again. Technically, that wouldn't even be correct. Her experience didn't extend much beyond kissing. Properly chaperoned, of course. The Old One had never permitted her to go out on a date alone.

Lynn didn't understand the handicap she was working under, but Jenny had no intention of telling her. It was too embarrassing. To be educated at a girls-only private high school was bad enough. But while Ben had been allowed to attend the University of British Columbia right here in Vancouver, she had been packed off to a women's college in Washington. The only boys she had met there were at chaperoned dances—for which they had been ordered in, like take-out food, from a nearby military academy. Try as she might, Jenny had found it impossible to picture any of them as a love match.

Jenny remembered how she had become a voracious reader of romance novels before she decided to try writing one herself. Scorning a word processor, she had written with a pen, shaping her characters just as the women of another century had done. Writing that first book had been a release. Finding that someone wanted to publish it had been heaven.

Nobody had criticized her love scenes then. Jenny thumped the couch with a clenched fist. How could one phone call make her feel so inadequate? Not only couldn't she meet a deadline, but now she couldn't write love scenes! *Ridiculous! I can do anything I set my mind to,* she told herself furiously.

Sarah was outraged. How dare he act like she was a common strumpet! She was a governess and contracted only for that service, thank you very much!

His gaze continued to move lazily over her, and she clutched her wrapper shut while hastening to pull the bedclothes up to her chin. "Get out of my bedroom," she ordered. He ignored her, a knowing glint in his eyes.

"Let me correct you. It's my *bedroom." He moved closer to the bed.*

"Get out!" Sarah repeated. "So long as your children are in my care, it's mine." Sir Randolph bent toward her, and Sarah warningly raised her hand. A resounding crack! *echoed across the room, and he pulled back hastily.*

Stupefied, Sarah stared at the angry red mark of her hand on his cheek. Sir Randolph, she could tell, was also confused.

* * *

Rats, Jenny thought miserably. *So am I.* She massaged her aching neck and stared at the page. It had been corrected so many times, she could hardly see what she had written. *I was wrong and Lynn was right,* she realized. *It's been a week and I still haven't managed it.* Sarah was as real to her as one of her family. But Sir Randolph was a ghost. Just how did she know what he felt when Sarah slapped his face? And where did she get off describing the knowing glint in his eye? Just what, pray tell, was it that he knew?

Jenny put her pen down, yawning loudly—rudely—something she would never have dared to do at home. She needed a break. Her gaze wandered to the tiny black-and-white television on the bookshelf, but she decided not to turn it on. She felt unavoidably guilty every time she watched the news and heard she was still missing.

A walk to the convenience store on the corner might cheer her up, she decided impulsively. And pizza would be a nice change from macaroni dinner—she'd worked hard today and she deserved a treat. Jenny stared, somewhat gloomily, at the blank pages sticking out from the manuscript. *Drat!* Those love scenes were going to be the death of her.

Jenny took her jacket and purse, leaving Sarah and Sir Randolph to cope as best they could by themselves. It was dark outside, but the stars were shining. She raised her head, exhilarated. A breeze caressed her hair, and Jenny thought of how far she had come. Unexpectedly, she felt a hand on her shoulder. She turned.

"Give me your purse." The man loomed large and threatening. His outstretched fingers threaded through the straps of her purse and tore it from her side in one jerking movement. Openmouthed, Jenny stared at him.

"No . . . you can't!" She grabbed suddenly at the purse, struggling to free it from his stronger grasp. All the money she had was in that purse! Refusing to let go, she found herself dragged across the sidewalk. Her feet scraped the edge of the curb as the man, with a final mighty wrench, yanked the purse forward and broke her hold. Jenny stumbled to her knees. She watched, stunned, as the man quickly merged with the shadows and disappeared.

Trembling, Jenny got up. Her hand probed for damage to her throbbing knees. She brushed off some gravel and stared fearfully at the inky blackness. The book had consumed all her attention for a week. She hadn't been shopping since her first hurried excursion to an all-night supermarket. All she had left in the apartment was a box of macaroni and a few withered apples. What could she do? Fleetingly, she thought of phoning the police. But her picture was still prominent on the daily news reports. They would just turn her over to her family, she realized.

Jenny's head drooped. Her eyes filled with tears,

and her gaze wandered over the silent buildings. She blinked. A bulletin board mounted on the glass front of an empty building caught her attention. An idea already forming in her mind, Jenny moved to stand in front of it. She searched among the flapping notices and found a new one, squarely mounted in the center of the board. *Help Wanted: Waitress Position.* The name of the restaurant was written in Cantonese. Jenny wiped her tears away with a shaky hand, and a look of determination settled on her face.

Two weeks later, Jenny was already feeling like a veteran. She swabbed tables and took down complicated orders with an enthusiasm that appalled most of the other staff members at the Jade Paradise. What was wrong with them? Jenny wondered. It was wonderful to have a job. Her family had never allowed her to work. It was tiring, she had to admit, but Jenny found she was enjoying the sensation of being pleasantly exhausted at night. It had brought her closer to her characters, she knew. She sympathized more readily with Sarah's despair at performing her endless round of tasks as a governess while waiting hopelessly for Sir Randolph to propose.

It was odd, she thought now as she scrubbed at a smear of dried ketchup on the lunch counter. The book was going remarkably well, though her day job had put drastic limits on the hours she could write. But her pen seemed to fly through the pages at night, and the manuscript was nearing completion. The only thing holding it back from the finish line was her continuing inability to cope with the love scenes.

"Stop that," Jin Sing complained. "You'll wear out the counter." The cook leaned forward in the order window that was his only view into the dining area of the restaurant and handed Jenny a plate. She moved nimbly—threading her way through the scattered tables was old hat by now—and promptly delivered it to table nine, occupied by an elderly man who brightened at the sight of his steaming dumplings.

Jenny returned to tackle the counter. Jin Sing kept telling her not to bother, but she was determined to do a good job. Bleach had restored the yellowing arborite to gleaming whiteness, and she intended to keep it that way.

The door jangled softly as two young men came in, joking and crowding their way to the lunch counter at the front of the restaurant. Wearing hooded jackets and tight jeans, they reeked of trouble. Jin Sing sensed it. His wrinkled face lifted to stare, frowning, from the order window.

The two men sat down at the counter, not seeming to notice that the other restaurant patrons were giving them a wide berth. One of them, a black, muscular man with a gold cross dangling from his right earlobe, eyed Jenny speculatively.

In her trim uniform—Jenny had insisted on pressing it when Jin Sing had turned it over to her—Jenny's slimness was immediately apparent. Its short, flaring skirt showed off her slender but well-muscled legs. The simple white shirt, stitched with the restaurant logo on its left pocket, made Jenny look more like a schoolgirl than a working adult.

"I'll have a cheeseburger and an orange soda," the black man said. "Anything else you want to give me, Hot Legs?"

Jenny flushed. She scribbled down his order and moved to leave, but he held out a massive arm to block her. "Not so fast, girl. My friend here wants something, too."

Jenny, feeling frightened, automatically flipped her pad to a new page. Last week there had been a fight in the restaurant. Other businesses in the area next to the waterfront were complaining, too. Tough young men—who looked prosperous, but had no visible employment—were changing what had been a relatively quiet place into a neighborhood where the residents were on edge.

Jenny looked fearfully at the other man, and her eyes widened. A shock that was almost electric ran through her, and the pad dangled unnoticed in her suddenly numb fingers. He was the biggest Chinese man she had ever seen. Over six feet four inches tall and smoothly muscled, he was a giant version of her own family members. His skin was so light that it had taken a healthy tan. His mouth looked sensitive. But his heavy black eyebrows were undeniably masculine, she thought. Along with the hard planes of his cheekbones, they gave him the look of a Mongol.

The stranger raised his head, and something fleeting passed over his face when he saw Jenny. It was quickly suppressed when he turned to answer a question from his companion. Jenny saw that his eyes, unusually, were not brown, but a deep amber. They glinted like those of a tiger.

"The lo mein . . . is it any good today?" he asked.

"It's always good," Jenny said automatically. "It's one of our best dishes." And it was, she knew. Old Jin Sing fussily chose the fresh noodles each morning from among the stalls at the Chinese food market.

"That, please."

With an effort, Jenny pulled herself from the penetrating gaze. "Did you want *cha*?" she asked in Cantonese.

"Tea would be fine," he said firmly in English with no trace of an accent. The black man slowly, teasingly, removed his arm to allow Jenny to pass.

Her thoughts were in a whirl as she stood on tiptoe to pass the orders through to Jin Sing. The cook grunted in approval when he saw the second ticket. "Hamburgers and chips," he had often complained to

Jenny. "It's all anyone ever seems to order. No sense of diet."

Jenny fled to the tiny cubicle of a washroom and kicked a box filled with paper napkins aside so she could study her reflection in the mirror. The face of a stranger stared back at her from the age-clouded glass of the mirror. Her face was uncharacteristically flushed, and her eyes were bright with excitement. Her heart gave little leaps like those of a puppy trying unsuccessfully to scramble onto a couch. How handsome he was! And how little she knew about him, she thought more soberly. Jenny, living alone, had grown more alert to the threat of danger. Every one of her senses was telling her now that these men were dangerous.

But there was something about the man with the amber eyes that was different, she thought. She didn't sense the same malice that she felt coming from his companion. Or was she just telling herself that? Jenny brushed her hair quickly, in short, jerking strokes. She patted a damp tissue across her feverish face. She had never looked better, she knew. And she had never felt worse.

When she returned to the restaurant, she noted with dismay that her orders were already piling up.

"Get a move on, will you?" Glenda hissed. "I've already cleaned two of your tables."

"I'll bet you took the tips too," Jenny couldn't help

retorting. She had little patience with Glenda, who had a habit of helping out with the other tables only when tipping customers were about to leave. Any money left on the tables inevitably disappeared into her apron pocket.

The redheaded waitress gave her an angry glance and hurriedly snatched up clean glasses and silverware. New and impatient customers were already seated at her tables.

Jenny waded into the thick of the lunch-hour rush with no time to spare on wondering about the man with the amber eyes.

She had served three tables in her section, brought a booster seat for a bright-eyed toddler, and made up six salads for a group of chattering women, their shopping bags clutched to their sides, when the order bell dinged once, signaling a counter order was ready.

Jenny retrieved the hamburger and lo mein and served the two men quickly, half anticipating and half fearing another thrilling look from those amber eyes. But the Chinese man did not raise his head. Embarrassed, Jenny suddenly realized she had forgotten their drinks.

What an amateur thing to do, she chided herself. They should have had them ten minutes ago. She got the soft drink and a pot of tea. She placed them in front of the men and hesitated. Then she poured a cup from the steaming teapot—a courtesy not normally extended at the busy restaurant—and placed it in front of the amber-eyed stranger. He took it, briefly thanking her.

Jenny's mind flew back to Edward and the unwelcome pressure of his fingers. The stranger had made no such move to touch her hand. Jenny felt oddly disappointed. The stranger's head rose, his eyes curious, and Jenny realized she was standing there like a fool, frozen in front of him. His eyes traveled without expression over her neat figure, checking her out from head to toe. Then he looked away, seemingly dismissing her.

Not so his friend. He made Jenny's life miserable for the next fifteen minutes, asking her for a date and speculating on what was under that short length of skirt. His companion remained silent, keeping one big hand curled around his teacup as he ate.

When they rose to leave, Jenny was torn between relief and panic. She felt ready to cry with frustration. Why was it that the men you didn't want to attract were invariably the ones you did?

She thought of Edward and her family, and a pang of homesickness struck at her heart. The misery on her face was impossible to conceal. Even the unobservant stranger noticed.

"Come on, Rocky. Let's get moving," he said quietly.

"You sure you don't want to come along with Rocky, Hot Legs?"

Jenny didn't respond. Rocky flung a Loonie at the counter. The dollar coin rolled to the floor, and Jenny made no move to pick it up. The black man winked at her. "More where that comes from, babe. Rocky be back." He strutted away, following the smooth gait of his tall friend.

Jenny stared at their departing backs, aghast. *Be back? Great,* she thought bitterly. She rushed to catch up with the rest of her orders. She had shamefully neglected her other customers since the stranger had shown up. But Jenny still found time to snatch a quick glimpse out the window to see where they were going. The two men, the one wide and black, the other tall and golden, crossed the street. They walked three doors down, turning into a shabby, one-story building between the barbershop and the laundromat.

Jenny made a face of distaste. It was the pool hall, a decrepit place where the too-well-dressed young men in the neighborhood were usually to be found. She had made the mistake of walking by there only once. Eyed by hard-looking youths who wolf-whistled as she passed, Jenny had since taken care to stick to the other side of the street.

After she served her tables and cleared three others, Jenny began to clean the counter, scrubbing halfheartedly at a coffee stain. For a moment, her hand curled around the teacup left by the stranger, sensing its fleeting warmth. She remembered the big fist his hand had made as it cradled the tiny cup. Then she returned the used dishes to the kitchen, inwardly scolding herself for being so silly. She dug furiously into the pots in the sink.

"Don't wear them out too," Jin Sing complained. He went back to chopping a bunch of fresh carrots into neatly slivered pieces.

"Do you know anything about him?" She blushed. "I mean them—those two men who were sitting at the counter?"

"Who?" The cook's thin face was momentarily puzzled. Then it hardened. "You mean that pair of hoodlums." He slammed the cleaver into the butcher's block.

"Hoodlums?"

Jin Sing's white shirt billowed out on his thin frame as he raised his hands to his wrinkled neck and jerked it in imitation of a hanging. "Gang members," he said in a hiss.

Jenny's heart gave an uncomfortable leap. "He— they can't be," she protested. "Not really."

"Yes," the cook insisted, his angular Adam's apple bobbing in indignation. "They're ruining this neighborhood." His eyes softened as he realized Jenny's innocence. "Not your kind at all," he added pointedly. "When is your family arriving to join you? They should not have let you come to this city alone."

"Soon," Jenny lied. "Once my mother's finished her treatment, the herbalists said my father will be able to bring her from Hong Kong."

"That will be good. Vancouver is a beautiful place—but not a place for a girl by herself to be picking up strange companions."

Jenny reddened. Was she that transparent, then? She turned back to attack the pots, scrubbing their dulled copper to a high gleam over the protests of the cook. She absently tilted one back and forth, musing that its tawny highlights were exactly the color of the stranger's eyes.

The rest of the shift dragged on. Only a few customers straggled in after six o'clock. Jenny's feet had begun to hurt—she had learned why most waitresses she had ever seen wore support hose and flat, comfortable-looking shoes—but she made no complaint when Jin Sing asked her to stay late and help him sweep the floors.

By the time they finished, it had grown nearly dark outside. "You should go home now," Jin Sing said. Satisfied, he surveyed the chairs neatly stacked upside down on each table. "I've kept you too late. The streets aren't safe for a girl like you after dark."

Jenny assured him that she would be careful and firmly rejected his kindly meant offer to escort her home. She wanted to be alone with her thoughts. Ever since she had seen the stranger, her mind had worried away at what bits she had gleaned, including Jin Sing's unsettling assertion that he was a gang member.

"I almost forgot." The cook dug into his pocket. "Today is payday."

Jenny smiled. Now she could pay her rent. The old woman who managed the apartment building had been reminding her daily that she was late. Delighted, Jenny realized that she had overcome another daunting obstacle—and all on her own, without any help from the family. It was lucky Jin Sing provided at least one meal a day for his waitresses, though. Without that, Jenny knew, she would have suffered a lot more than work-roughened hands.

"Thank you!" she sang out. She impulsively planted a kiss on the old cook's cheek. He stumbled back, blinking, and then smiled at her excitement.

"Get going now," he said sternly. "It's almost dark." Jenny scurried outside after putting the check in her purse. The cook locked the door after her.

The night was warm, one of those drawn-out summer nights so inviting it seemed a shame to sleep. The stars suddenly trembled, and Jenny's quick eyes noted that one of them was flashing to the ground. Hastily, she made a wish. *I wish for him to notice me,* she thought wistfully.

Jenny crossed the street, feeling apprehensive as she

neared the pool hall. *This is dumb,* she thought. *But I just want to see if he's still inside.* She hesitated as she drew close to the smoked-glass window and squinted to see inside. A thin form broke free of the shadows at the door. It chuckled as Jenny turned apprehensively to see who it was.

She recognized him and suddenly felt sick. It was one of the creeps who made the pool hall his second home. Pasty-faced and about nineteen years old, he was usually attached to the group who habitually shouted catcalls at Jenny from across the street. She began to back away.

"Get paid today?" the teenager asked, his long face alight with interest. "I was watching you and that old Chink through the window." His arm lashed out and cold fingers dug into her shoulder. "Maybe you and me should go party."

Jenny began to scream, but the teenager planted a hard hand against her mouth and an arm around her waist. A shaft of light shot out against their struggling bodies as the door of the pool hall opened. Jenny felt herself suddenly torn from the teenager's grip. She watched, stunned, as a powerful shove sent him flying into the street. The teenager got up angrily and stared at the Chinese man, noting his immense size. Then, cursing under his breath, he moved resentfully away.

"Are you okay?"

Jenny wordlessly nodded her head. Confused, she

moved away and then stumbled as her heel caught the curb. The stranger's arm shot out to rescue her for a second time. Jenny could almost swear he held her for a moment longer than necessary.

"Look here . . . I'd better walk you home," he said gruffly. "What's your boss thinking of? This is a dangerous neighborhood after dark."

This time, Jenny thought she could detect the hint of an accent. "Thank you," she said in Cantonese. "That would be very nice."

The stranger made no reply as he fell into step beside her. She remembered uneasily that she knew nothing about him. But recklessly, Jenny decided that she didn't care. "My name is Jenny," she said in English. "What's yours?"

"Mine is Lukas." He looked down at her quickly, but offered no last name. "How long have you worked at the Jade Paradise?"

"Just two weeks now." Jenny peered up at her unexpected escort, trying to see his face in the deepening dusk.

"That explains why I haven't seen you before," he said, half to himself. "I've been out of town for three weeks."

"Oh? Where?"

"Just away," he said with an impatient twist of his head. "You sure ask a lot of questions."

Abashed, Jenny ducked her head.

"I didn't mean it like that," he said quietly. "Sorry if I was rude."

"It's okay. I *do* ask a lot of questions. I've got a lot to learn."

"Why's that?" he asked, eyeing her.

It was Jenny's turn to be evasive. "It's . . . a new city to me," she improvised. "I've got to learn everything." Hesitantly, Jenny told him the same story she had concocted for Jin Sing. She hated to lie to him. But there was too much at stake, she told herself. How could she be sure he would not turn her in for the reward her family was offering?

"When will your family arrive?"

"In a month," she said. She lowered her eyes. That was another lie on her conscience, she thought guiltily. They reached the concrete steps of her apartment building, and Jenny turned to thank him.

"This where you live?" Lukas looked surprised. And was that concern on his face?

"I know it doesn't look like much," she said stoutly, "but it's safe. Thanks for your help. I won't be so foolish again."

She stared at his broad shoulders and tanned face, fully revealed in the harsh glow of the overhead light. In return, his tawny eyes dipped to study her slim form. Jenny felt him looking at her hands as she dug into her pocket for the key.

She turned slightly to shield them from his gaze.

There was a blister on her ringless left hand that contrasted oddly with the sensitive long fingers. It was a dead giveaway that she had never done rough work before.

Had he seen through her story? His eyes looked disbelieving. But lots of Chinese women worked in restaurants—he couldn't possibly know who she was. He stared at her until Jenny began to grow uncomfortable.

"Would you like to go out for a bite sometime?" he asked finally.

"What about your friend?" she asked quickly.

His eyes darkened. "Don't worry about Rocky. I'll keep him in line."

"In that case . . . yes."

"How about tomorrow?"

"After work? I get off at six on Fridays."

"Sure. I'll be by here at eight, then."

He stood, quietly staring at her for another long moment. Then he turned and strode off the way he had come.

Jenny watched him go, her head pulsing with excitement. *Finally!* Someone she was interested in had asked her out. He couldn't be a gang member, she told herself firmly. Would a gang member have rescued her? Jin Sing must be wrong.

Her heart light, Jenny began to fly up the stairs to her apartment—and to her book. She would have to write quickly to make up for working late tonight and going out tomorrow.

She stopped, suddenly aghast and then amused. *Why, I forgot . . . I never asked him what he does for a living.*

He did seem to have a mesmerizing effect on her, she mused dreamily. It was like the world around her had disappeared onto a different plane of existence and she was left only with him. Jenny smiled, suddenly thoughtful, and sprang up the rest of the stairs. Perhaps she could take another crack at those love scenes tonight.

Chapter Three

"What's the matter with you? That's the second time you've gotten the orders wrong."

Jenny started. "I'm sorry," she told Jin Sing. "I guess my mind was wandering."

"Well, tell it to wander back to the lunch counter," he said fiercely. "This is a competitive business since that Greek restaurant relocated two doors down."

Jenny swiftly exchanged the mixed-up orders and apologized to her customers for the delay. The elderly Chinese woman who came in daily for a bowl of noodles patted her hand. The Nigerian student grunted without raising his head from his textbook. Really, what was she thinking of? How could anyone get a hamburger mixed up with a bowl of noodles? She would have to try harder, she thought, but she *was* finding it hard to concentrate.

Her date was tonight, she remembered happily for the hundredth time. What should she wear? She had brought so few clothes with her, and she had no money to buy new things. She thought longingly of her bulging closet at home, with its dozens of dresses and neatly laid-out shoes.

An elbow jabbed into her ribs, and Jenny grunted with pain. "Get moving," Glenda said impatiently. "Don't leave me with the lunch hour rush by myself."

"But that way you'd be able to take *all* the tips," Jenny fired back.

Glenda reddened to the tips of her auburn hair. "Think you're hot stuff, don't you? I've been waitressing here for months and *I* think you stink. Why don't you go back to Hong Kong?"

"Get to work! Both of you!"

Jin Sing slammed his cleaver into the butcher block. The two women dove through the kitchen doors and back to their tables. Jenny couldn't resist thumbing her nose at Glenda, but the waitress had already turned to speak to a customer.

She had cleared two window tables and was carrying a tray of dirty dishes from a third when Rocky came into the restaurant. Jenny fled to the kitchen and put the dishes in the sink. She hung back in the doorway, hoping the black man wouldn't see her.

"What's *wrong* with you today?" the cook demanded. "Get out there!"

At least the counter was between them, Jenny told herself. Unfortunately, Rocky was sitting in her section. She looked hopefully around, but there was no sign of Lukas. She reluctantly pulled out her pad.

"Hey, Hot Legs. What's good today?"

Rocky was trying to be nice, she thought, terrified. She edged closer to take his order. It was like passing a pit bull and wondering how long its chain was, she decided grimly. "Everything," she said weakly.

"I'll take a cheeseburger and an orange soda."

Jenny wondered if he ever ate anything else. She went to the order window and tacked the order up. She stayed away from the counter, clearing tables and serving customers by the windows until she heard the order bell ding. She dropped the plate in front of Rocky and turned to escape.

"You want to hit the town with me tonight?" Rocky had taken off his jacket. He was wearing a sleeveless T-shirt that showed off his muscles. He flexed them now, confident of her answer.

"No."

Rocky's jaw dropped. "Babe . . . don't you know who I am?" He lowered his voice to a growl. "Nobody can show you a good time like Rocky."

Jenny felt sickened. "I have a date already," she said. But Rocky had already turned from her and was eyeing Glenda. Jenny thankfully scurried away. Jin Sing asked her to fetch a carton of napkins, and by the time she returned, Glenda and Rocky were standing together by the door. Glenda was fingering a clump of her wiry hair and smiling.

She turned away, hearing Glenda's squeaky laugh and Rocky's deep chuckle before the door jangled shut. When the freckled waitress clumped to the back to fetch some plates, Jenny couldn't help speaking. "You'd go out with that guy?"

"Sure—wouldn't you?"

"No."

Glenda's face grew sullen, and she turned her back to Jenny. She didn't speak to her for the rest of the shift. Jenny didn't care, but she kept a watchful eye on her tips. If Glenda was crazy enough to go out with a guy like that, she wasn't going to worry about her, she thought with disgust. She had better things to think about.

Jenny drove an impatient hand through her freshly washed hair. Just what was she going to put on? For a moment she thought crazily of sneaking home to get something stunning to wear. But then she remembered the dress she had worn the night she fled home. She discovered it pushed back and forgotten at the very back of the tiny closet.

Thankfully, Jenny held it up to her cheek. It was a

beautiful dress, fashioned of Japanese silk as smooth as water. The dark green dress was one of her favorites. Flocked with tiny bits of white spun silk and cut in a simple wraparound style, the minidress was at once form-revealing and subtle. Her eyes sparkling, Jenny put it on and adjusted the wide fabric belt. She tied it, letting the silk tassels dangle free. She twirled once in front of the cheap mirror tacked to the closet door. The belt emphasized her tiny waist. The color complemented her flawless skin. Her eyes stood out like black pearls against the rich fabric.

Jenny dove back into the closet and retrieved her sandals. Luckily, they were white and somewhat dressy because of their high heels and intricately woven straps. After putting them on, Jenny next regarded her hair. What could she do that was different? She scooped up her mass of raven black hair and twisted it round and round, pinning the coiled length to the top of her head. She turned her head critically from side to side, deciding she liked the effect. Her eyes brightened with excitement.

Where would he take her? she wondered. Her face fell as she remembered the pool hall. Not there, surely. Her chin rose indignantly. *If he does*, she thought, *I'll just leave*.

Jenny hurriedly touched a dark raspberry gloss to her mouth. Her lips widened, growing luscious as ripe berries. A dusting of dark blush to emphasize the jutting wings of her cheekbones came next. Jenny thought she looked a bit tired. The nights of writing until all hours were beginning to take their toll. She patted a light concealing cream on the shadows below her eyes. Then she picked up a navy blue eye pencil and outlined her eyes. She brushed on two coats of mascara—waiting for the first coat to dry before applying the second—and her eyes were transformed into pools of brightness.

Unlike her uniform, the dress had no pockets. What could she use for a purse? Jenny's gaze wandered across the room and seized on her white leather pencil case. It was overlarge and sported a brass symbol—a stylized *J* and *L* on the front. It would make a dandy clutch purse, she decided. Upending it, she carelessly dumped its contents out onto her manuscript. She filled it with her lip gloss, comb, a perfume stick, and tissue instead.

Jenny flew down the stairs, right on time. She stood in the foyer for a nervous fifteen minutes. He wasn't coming, she decided for the third time. She was about to return to her apartment—where she knew she would fling herself down on the couch and squander a perfectly good evening feeling sorry for herself instead of writing—when Lukas suddenly appeared, jogging easily from around the corner.

"Sorry I'm late." His eyes moved appreciatively from the crown of her shining head to work their way down the rounded lines of her slender figure. "I got tied up . . . with business."

What business? Jenny was about to ask eagerly. But Lukas smiled, exposing even white teeth, and the question faded from her mind. He wasn't wearing jeans, she was pleased to see. He had on a linen suit and looked twice as good as she had remembered. Feeling relieved, she mentally crossed the pool hall off the list of places she had speculated he might take her for a date. Her arm tingled as he took it, urging her forward. "Come on," he said. "We'll just be on time if we hurry."

On time for what? she wondered. She lengthened her strides to match his giant gait, finding it a unique sensation. Ordinarily, she was forever trying to take smaller steps to match the shorter pace of her family members. Lukas rushed her along for ten minutes, turning first down side streets and then, to Jenny's growing dismay, back alleys. She was soon bewildered and unaware of where they were. A slat-thin cat sprang out with a strangled cry from behind a garbage can and Jenny shrank back, eyeing its mangled ears.

The salty smell of the sea was growing stronger. She wondered hopefully if he was taking her to a waterfront café.

"We're almost there." Lukas stepped nimbly past a jumble of overturned cartons and pallets. "Sorry about the shortcut." He drew Jenny around a crumbling brick corner and she blushed. She was over-whelmingly conscious of the firm grip of his hand.

She gasped. They were at the edge of the harbor, just down from the moorage of one of Vancouver's yacht clubs. Forested mountains stood out in rugged relief to the north, while the inlets and bays in the west and south gleamed a vibrant green in the golden glow of the setting sun. But it was not the considerable beauty of the placid harbor scene that had caused Jenny's gasp.

Directly in front of her wondering eyes was a Chinese junk. Its flags twisted merrily in the ocean breeze. As on any self-respecting junk, two narrow slotted eyes were painted on its soaring square prow. Jenny felt close to tears. *I haven't seen one of those since . . . since we left Hong Kong,* she realized. She looked quickly at Lukas, realizing he had believed her story of arriving recently. He was trying to cure her homesickness! She felt a rush of warmth, not all of it gratitude for his kind act. Blushing, Jenny realized she felt guilty for lying to him.

''There's more.'' His hand reached for hers, and she thrilled again at the touch of his flesh as he led her to the gangplank. The deck of the ship was full—not with the bales or cartons or coils of rope she expected to see—but with tiny elegant tables perched daintily on the carpeted deck. Each was laid with a white damask tablecloth and bore a fresh bouquet of chrysanthemums.

She turned to Lukas, her eyes shining. "It's beautiful."

"It's a restaurant I thought you might appreciate. People tell me it reminds them of Hong Kong."

"Oh, it does," Jenny hastened to reassure him. She felt nostalgia sweep over her as she studied the eyes of the junk. She remembered curling up at the feet of the Old One as a child and demanding to know why the boats had eyes. The Old One's explanation—that the boats needed them to see where they were going— had made perfect sense to her child's mind. She felt a moment's sadness. Life had been less complicated then.

A maître d' met them at the top of the gangplank. Lukas whispered to him, announcing a name that she couldn't quite catch, and the tuxedoed figure beamed. He led them to a table—surely the choicest on the deck, Jenny noted with growing appreciation—at the very tip of the jutting prow. It was about four feet higher than the others on the deck below, and lightly screened off from the rest of the diners by a fall of dangling vines.

Once they were seated, Jenny realized they were in their own private world. The table looked out over the gently lapping waters and the sinking sun. Enchanted, she twisted on the cushions of the built-in seat to stare at the seagulls bobbing lazily on the waters below. Impulsively, she took a roll from the table and threw a bit of the bread in the water. The seagulls were suddenly all business, fighting greedily for their share of the unexpected bounty.

''Would you like to feed the fish?''

''What—?''

''The fish—come on, I'll show you.'' Lukas scooped up two rolls. He parted the fall of vines and, following him, Jenny soon realized that a section of the deck below had been removed and a fish pond installed. Giant goldfish—carp—swam lazily back and forth, their transparent tails and fins trailing behind like gauzy veils.

Jenny knelt and studied the humorously pop-eyed fish. Lukas divided a roll in half and gave it to Jenny. Avid as the greedy seagulls, the carp turned toward her as Lukas passed her the bread and dashed in a mad rush for the water's edge. A dozen eyes peeped at her as the fish bobbed up and down in the gently rippling water. ''This is great,'' Jenny said. She laughed to see how quickly they devoured the bread she scattered in front of their noses.

Lukas bent down beside her. She studied him shyly, liking his clear laugh when the largest carp of them all, a grandfather of some two feet, shook his whiskers at the temerity of a smaller fish that darted in to take the bread he had thrown.

Lukas was wearing a subtly darker tie with his cream-colored linen suit. *His clothes look expensive,* she thought, and she remembered again that she hadn't asked him what he did for a living. She opened her mouth, but his amber eyes, glowing as they rested on her, seduced her attention. She felt the heat of his gaze through the thin material of her dress. She wondered about the unusual color of his eyes. Conscious of his nearness, she dropped her gaze furtively to admire the long, muscled span of his thighs. She looked away, her heart beating strongly, and banished the nagging memory of Edward to the very back of her mind.

Jenny rose gracefully from her crouch and brushed the crumbs from her lap. She laughed as the fish raced to the edge, hoping to win a last fragment. Lukas got up too and captured her hand. She smiled at him as they returned to their table and sank into the comfortable cushions.

''Sorry I rushed you, but I didn't want you to miss a moment of the sunset,'' he said. ''Look''—he pointed to the mountains—''can you see it?''

Jenny watched as the rays of the sinking sun caught the highest peaks in a rosy dance of lights. The illumination was unworldly, almost holy, and she caught her breath at the sight. The peaks were golden now, then red-gold, and finally shadowed with the coming darkness.

''That was wonderful.'' She reached for his hand

and squeezed it gratefully. "How did you ever hear about this place?"

"I get around," he said easily. "With so many people coming from Hong Kong, someone decided it might be a hit."

"It is with me," Jenny said, and then she blushed. Would he think her totally unsophisticated for being so easy to please? Jenny straightened—not an easy thing to do because the soft cushions were coaxing her to sink back—and tried to look more worldly: like a woman who was taken out to dine at exotic places every night of the week. Lukas grinned at her, and Jenny suddenly knew he wasn't taken in by her new pose. She shrugged softly and relaxed.

The waiter appeared with bowls of steaming water and a miniature silver candelabra. He lit the candles, and Jenny realized how dark it was getting. A string of lights threaded on the ropes overhead flashed on. *I'm not in heaven,* she thought delightedly. *This is more like being in fairyland.*

They dipped their hands in the scented water, drying them afterward on soft cloths held out by the waiter. In a matter of minutes, a bewildering variety of dishes appeared on the table. Jenny was hungry, and the food was wonderful; as good as Hong Kong's best. An artful display of whiskered prawns—real prawns, not the big shrimp that Vancouver restaurants more commonly served—skirted by snow peas and seasoned with cracked peppercorns, was delicious. And she could hardly pass up the fragrant sesame chicken with its colorful garnish of red peppers arranged in a flaring circle. What a difference it made when you weren't serving the food, she thought. Probably nobody appreciated being waited on more than a waitress, she realized.

"Enough," she said at last. But the waiter had returned yet again, drawn to the table by a sharp gesture from Lukas.

"No," he said firmly. "You have to try this dessert."

Groaning, she agreed. "But that's it," she insisted. "I don't think I'll be able to walk after this as it is."

He laughed heartily. His smile parted to reveal a glint of white teeth that glowed in the candlelight.

The waiter returned shortly with chocolate-dipped kiwifruit and an exquisite hard sauce. It was delicious. Jenny was scraping up the last of the chocolate when she felt Lukas staring at her. "Aren't you going to save some for me?" he asked wickedly.

Jenny halted in midscrape. Mortified, she realized it was a dessert for *two*. She wanted to sink under the comfortable seating and die. The weeks of subsisting on plain rice and handouts from the restaurant had played her false.

"You must think I'm an awful pig," she said

gloomily. "My family would be horrified if they saw me eating like that in public."

He laughed hugely. "Don't they eat? And anyway, you eat like a little bird."

"A little vulture maybe," rejoined Jenny. "My gosh, how will I ever squeeze back into my uniform?"

"You've got chocolate on your mouth," he noted absently. Jenny wiped at her mouth with her napkin and scrubbed briskly at the corner of her bow-shaped lips. "That still hasn't got it," he said, his voice suddenly teasing. He bent and kissed her, his tongue sliding gently to the corner of her mouth, tasting the chocolate.

Begun half-jokingly, the kiss subtly deepened. Jenny stiffened, knowing she should draw back, but she seemed unable to quell the urgent pounding in her veins. He pulled her toward him, and Jenny felt herself slip easily across the cushions and into his arms. His lips grew more insistent, and his strong hands slid up to grip her elbows gently, urging her into the kiss—into an exploding world of delights. She kissed back, discovering a hunger deep inside herself that had nothing to do with food. His lips drew away from hers reluctantly and returned to them for a final, driven kiss before he released her.

Jenny stared at him, dazed.

"I always did like chocolate," he said, looking deeply into her eyes.

"I—I never liked it quite that much before," Jenny said. She giggled shakily. He stared at her a moment longer and then rose, his long legs hardening with muscle.

"Come on, we'll be late," he said.

Now what? Jenny was bemused. Lukas was full of surprises, moving at an unexpected pace that made her feel like she was out of her depth. The meal alone would have kept her happy for days, she thought. She fixed a strand of hair that had come loose, her arms rising delicately in what she was unaware was a provocative gesture.

"You're the most unlikely waitress I've ever seen," Lukas said suddenly.

Jenny stiffened. She was afraid to say anything. She felt relieved when he did not pursue the topic further. She picked up her pencil case.

The maître d' bowed to Lukas as they mounted the step to the gangplank. Jenny turned to him. "Don't we have to pay?" she asked worriedly.

Her eyes widened as she saw Lukas slip a small package to the man. The maître d' quickly put it out of sight, concealing it in an inside pocket of his tuxedo. "It's no problem," Lukas told her smoothly. "It's all arranged."

Arranged? Jenny wondered what that meant. She stared back at the junk as they hurried along the wharf. The maître d', standing like a sentinel at the top of the gangplank, was outlined blackly against the soft gray of the night. What had Lukas given him? The package was too large to be a few bills and too small to be a letter. The warm glow inspired by the kisses began to fade, and Jenny felt her misgivings begin to grow.

Lukas noticed her change of mood. "Something wrong?" he asked ironically.

"No . . . no. It's just . . . what did you give him?"

Lukas frowned. "That's business," he said abruptly.

But Jenny was worried now. She studied Lukas, noting the thick-edged eyebrows that stood out starkly against his smoothly chiseled features. They were the eyebrows of a predator. *He looks like a man who takes what he wants,* she thought. "What do you do for a living?" she dared to ask. He stopped abruptly and released Jenny's hand from his grasp.

"What's wrong? Has someone been telling you that I'm in with the wrong crowd?" His eyes looked golden in the dark. They stared, unblinking, directly into her own. For some reason, Jenny felt he was measuring her—judging her and finding her wanting. She felt like a foolish schoolgirl.

"I have heard that." Jenny overcame her embarrassment and stared right back at him.

Lukas was watching her intently, his eyes glinting like those of a tiger about to leap. "Do you believe it?"

"I . . . no," Jenny admitted. Lukas relaxed. His eyes lost their intensity, and he pulled Jenny to him, kissing her solidly on the lips. Her heart sang, and the nagging doubt was stilled.

"I'm having the hardest time not doing that," Lukas said with a grin. "Come on, now." He recaptured her hand and urged her into a trot.

What next? Jenny thought again. She hurried to keep up with his lengthening stride. They were soon in the Gastown area. At this time of the evening, it meant a journey through a bewildering variety of people. Everyone in the world seemed to be out for an evening's fun. Jenny found herself gaping as Lukas drew her through the crowd. One woman, her hair dyed orange and laced with tiny black ribbons, was strolling with her date—a man with copper rings piercing the flesh of his upper arms. An Andean pipe band was serenading passersby from a lighted corner. A wiry street performer on the next street entertained a crowd with a juggling act that included bowls, cutlery, and lit flashlights.

Lukas stopped at last in front of a red-painted door. At least, Jenny thought it was red. The door was largely obscured under a tattered collection of autographed posters featuring rock bands and singers. It seemed familiar somehow. With a start, Jenny realized where they were. Lukas noticed her consternation and misread it.

"It's okay," he said. "This place is safe . . . and I'll make sure no one bothers you." His eyes flared hotly, and he drew Jenny to him, planting a kiss on her up-turned face. She pulled away.

"I . . . I don't really like rock music."

"You'll like this band," Lukas promised. "Everyone says they're on their way up." Certainly, the size of the gathered crowd seemed to indicate they were, Jenny thought, suddenly pleased. She moved to walk to the end of the block, where the lineup of restless people ended. Lukas pulled her back. He looked sharply at the burly doorman, who was chewing gum, one tattooed hand on his hip, and the other holding firmly onto the rope.

He spotted Lukas, and his face lit up in a beatific smile. "Hey, Lukas . . . go on in." A chorus of boos rose from the dozens of waiting couples, and the bouncer hastily turned back. "Knock it off, you animals," he shouted. He threatened them with a meaty arm.

Lukas opened the door and ushered Jenny inside. Her hands flew to her ears. The music and the roar of the crowd inside were deafening. She blinked, her eyes dazzled by the overhead lights. Lukas pushed past a tight knot of chattering girls who giggled and poked each other when they saw him. All of them looked too young to be at a nightclub. Their faces fell remarkably flat when they spotted his hand locked around Jenny's.

One, a petite girl with her hair teased into frizzy spikes, turned her back abruptly. Her haughty blond head tipped forward, whispering, and Jenny had no doubt she was saying something unflattering about her to her friends.

The rock club was small, but there seemed to be hundreds of people crowded into its cramped quarters. Practically everything in the club was red, she noticed. Lukas led her across a dance floor, its oak planks polished to a high gloss, and onto a set of red stairs. The wall mirrors were tinted, reflecting the people as dark shapes. A bewildering display of lights overhead caught Jenny's attention. She looked up, realizing that the ceiling was mirrored too, reflecting the lights strung on the stairs below.

"Lukas, my man!" Another hefty man—this one so huge he couldn't relax his arms against his sides— appeared.

"Did you save me a table?"

"Sure thing. A few more minutes, though, and you would have lost it." He slammed his fist into his hand, and the chains on his leather vest jangled. "This band is *hot*."

His eyes traveled over Jenny, and he whistled appreciatively. He ushered them up the stairs to a booth perched above the stage. He plucked the RESERVED sign from the table. "Enjoy," he said. "Best seats in the house."

It would be impossible not to see the band clearly from their table. More importantly Jenny thought, as she slouched down in the seat, it would be impossible for the band not to see *her*. It was no good, she realized with dismay. Not for the first time, she found herself wishing she wasn't so tall. Anyone in the band would be able to see her clearly if they happened to look in her direction.

"What would you like to drink?" Lukas asked. Startled, Jenny looked at him. The barmaid, dressed in a glittering halter dress of spangled stars, was standing at the table and tapping her foot impatiently.

"Anything. A . . . a soft drink would be fine," she said hastily. After the barmaid left, Lukas leaned forward.

"You are old enough to drink, aren't you?" he asked teasingly.

"I'm twenty-two," Jenny said absently, absorbed in staring at the empty stage. How was she ever going to get out of this one?

"I'm twenty-eight," Lukas told her. "I was born here. Don't you love Vancouver? There's so much to do here; I never get tired of it."

With an effort, Jenny pulled her eyes from the stage and smiled at Lukas. "Sure, I like it . . . of course, I haven't seen very much of it yet," she added hastily, remembering that she was supposed to be a new arrival.

Looking about the club, Jenny suddenly realized she did feel like a new arrival. There was so little she had been allowed to do. Even shopping was something she did in the company of her mother or a household servant. With the exception of summer vacations, she had never really been anywhere, if she didn't count her college years in the United States. She looked at the women seated at the tables below. Most of them were half-naked, dressed in a glittering array of abbreviated tight dresses and sophisticated evening wear. She looked down at her own softly clinging dress. *I must look like an overdressed baby,* she thought unhappily.

"You'll grow to love it here," Lukas promised her. "Wait till I show you Stanley Park." His eyes brightened. "I know a very romantic spot."

His arm, outstretched comfortably on the vinyl top of the booth, slid downward. Jenny felt a strange sense of déjà vu as his grip tightened around her and he bent forward to kiss her neck. She shivered, feeling the warm sensation of his lips against her skin. She raised her head to meet his and was rewarded by the sudden press of his lips on her own. Her senses reeled as he drew closer. His hands slid to her waist, enclosing its tiny span, and the kiss grew more urgent.

This is the real thing, she told herself dazedly. No wonder her love scenes had been flat and uninspired. She found herself eagerly kissing him back. After an eternity, Lukas raised his head and looked down at her with amazement. "Wow!" was all he said.

The whine of an electric guitar struck up, and Jenny flinched. She had forgotten where she was. She sat up hurriedly and then shrank back down. The band members were coming onstage, she saw, picking their way familiarly through the closet-high speakers and snaking electrical cords.

And then she saw him. Like the others, he was dressed in jeans and a Snow Tigers T-shirt. But his height and his way of standing—one moment self-assured and the next self-conscious—were unmistakable. His head was down as he fiddled with the bar on his guitar, intent on getting the instrument into perfect tune.

Jenny crouched lower in the seat and edged away from Lukas. She craned her neck behind a pillar. The band began its first song, striking up the opening chords of "Tina Tender" to a roar of approval from the crowd. Jenny knew it well. How many hours had she spent watching him work out the lyrics and listening to his dream that it would be the kind of song to make a big splash with a record company?

"This is a great song," Lukas said, misreading her strained interest. Jenny watched as the Snow Tigers' lead vocalist started into the lyrics, and the crowd hushed. His perfect tenor rang out clearly, caressing the words. The other band members, deeper-voiced, filled in with the chorus: "Tender to me, tender to touch; Tina, I love you, I need you so much."

He had been so proud of landing this gig, Jenny remembered. He had shown her the press photos of the club, its famous dance floor and its famous front door—once published on the cover of an international rock magazine. Dozens of famous musicians had gotten their first real break at the popular club and left their spray-painted signatures on the door in silent tribute. "I'll get mine on there someday, too," he had told her, his eyes shining.

He was really good, Jenny thought proudly. She couldn't resist ducking from behind the pillar to take a quick look. He flinched, fumbling a chord of the musical accompaniment before recovering. Dismayed, she realized that Ben had seen her. His face was frozen where before it had been animated. The rest of the song was flawless, but his eyes remained riveted on Jenny.

Lukas stirred beside her as the band began their next number. His eyebrows dove together in a single uncompromising line, and he seemed to grow even larger as he sat. "You know that guy?"

"Uh . . . I have to go to the washroom," Jenny said, ignoring his surprise. "Excuse me." She grabbed for her pencil-case clutch and fled. Her brother jerked again, but doggedly kept on singing.

Caught in the milling crowd below, Jenny asked a

waitress where the washroom was. She followed her quick gesture to a door scribbled with neon graffiti and let her breath out with a sigh of relief once she was safely behind it.

The blond girl who had earlier turned her back to Jenny was inside. She was standing, somewhat unsteadily, in front of the mirror and recoating her pale lips with a violent shade of scarlet lipstick. She tossed her blond, spiked head and grudgingly moved aside to make room for Jenny.

''I've never seen Lukas with a Chinese girl before,'' she said. Her eyes scrambled busily over Jenny, taking in her simple but expensive dress.

''Oh?'' Jenny said. Her thoughts were in a whirl. How was she to explain her brother to Lukas? And worse, how was she to explain Lukas to her brother?

Jenny fumbled through the pencil case for her gloss and touched it to her lips. Her eyes were wide and frightened, lending her a vulnerability that the blond girl thought she recognized.

''I'm Samantha,'' she said. ''Funny I haven't seen you before. It seems like I've been working for Lukas almost forever. Before that I was a runner for Rocky— but believe me, Lukas is a lot easier to take.''

The girl had the glazed eyes of a doll. High on her cheeks, Jenny saw, were two angry-looking fever spots. Whatever was she talking about? Jenny replaced her gloss in its case and wondered what she should do next. Now that Ben had seen her, it wouldn't be so easy to disappear again. The best thing she could do was to talk to him, she decided. Surely she could convince him not tell the family where she was.

"I know Lukas *very* well," the girl emphasized, her blue eyes narrowing. "Don't think the rest of us haven't tried to get special deals. Believe me, it won't work."

Inexplicably, Samantha pulled out a small plastic bag filled with white powder. "Want some?" she asked as companionably as if she were offering Jenny a stick of gum.

Jenny stepped backward, appalled. Samantha's babyish features hardened, and for an instant she looked years older than she had seemed a moment before. "Just remember," Samantha said, "Lukas doesn't have any time for runners who aren't producing. New customers are everything in this business." Her voice slurred. "Anyway, I saw him first," she mumbled.

Jenny flew out of the bathroom faster than she had gone in. Everyone was up and wandering about now that the band was taking a break between sets. Feeling dazed, she stood unmoving in the thick of the crowd. A sharp elbow poked her, and she pushed back reflexively, her gaze unseeing. Her heart, betrayed, beat convulsively. Lukas had lied.

Jenny felt as though she were going to be sick. His

soft kisses and caresses meant nothing now. Lukas had lied.

"Jenny! It is you . . . I thought I was dreaming. Are you all right?" Ben grasped her arm, his warm brown eyes exactly on a level with her own, and looked searchingly at her face. "Where have you been? The Old One's been half out of her mind with worry. We thought you'd been kidnapped."

Jenny's tears spilled over, and she collapsed into her brother's arms. "Ben . . . get me out of here."

"I can't, Jenny. Not yet. The next set is about to start. Look—why don't I call the family?"

"Oh, no," she said, digging her fingers into his arm. "Don't do that. Isn't there somewhere I can wait until you're finished?" *And be safe,* she wanted to add. *Safe to nurse my aching heart.*

"Sure. We've got a dressing room." His arm protectively wrapped around his sister, Ben led her to the back of the club. Jenny caught the darkly reflected anger of a face in the mirrored wall. She twisted her head to see Lukas standing upright in the balcony section, looming above them like a wrathful god. He stared down at them, his eyes burning. Jenny's steps faltered.

"Oh, hurry," she said with a moan. "This is so horrible."

Once she was safely locked in the dressing room and her brother had returned to his band, Jenny let go.

She cried and cried, while the disguising thump of the bass speakers pushed against the walls. How could she be so stupid? Her family was right. The old ways were the best ways. If it took an arranged marriage to keep someone as foolish as herself out of trouble, then so be it. Her family, at least, was doing its best to look out for her. Her own attempts to take care of things for herself were just one big mess.

The last set seemed to go on forever. Jenny washed her face and then sat down to hold her pounding head. When her brother returned, calling to her through the door, she jumped up to let him in. The other band members filed in after him. They stared at her curiously for a moment, but then glanced away. They were all Chinese and would not pry into a family affair that was none of their concern.

"Come on," Ben said. "The guys will take care of my equipment for me. Let's get you home. Are you cold?" He draped his jacket over her shoulders and led her to the staff entrance. Jenny snuggled closer to her brother, taking comfort from his protective warmth.

Ben's cream-colored Ferrari was parked out back. He began fishing his keys out of his pocket. Unexpectedly, a man stepped from the alley darkness. It was Lukas.

"First time I ever had someone ditch me halfway through the night," he said through clenched teeth.

His physical presence was overpowering, and Jenny turned her face against her brother's shoulder. She never wanted to see him again.

"I should have known . . . is it because he's got a Ferrari? Or are you just a music lover"—he said this scathingly—"one of those little girls willing to put out for a song and a party?"

"Who is this guy, Jenny?" Her brother was warily gauging the immense size of the stranger.

"It's okay," Lukas said, his angry demeanor relaxing. "You weren't who I thought you were. Go with him, if that's what you want."

Jenny was suddenly angry. What right did he have to speak to her like that? He was a criminal, the lowest of the low.

"Filth!" she said. She spat decisively at his feet. Lukas's face turned a remarkable shade of purple. Jenny feared for a moment that he would lunge forward, but instead his features changed to stone as he considered her taunt.

"So that's what you think? I—Never mind." He turned abruptly and went back into the club without a second look. Jenny, frozen to the spot, felt crazily that she had somehow wronged him. She was brought back to the present by her brother, who was tugging impatiently at her arm.

"Get moving, Jenny. I want to get out of here before your big friend comes back. Just what have you been up to, anyway?''

Ben bundled her into the car, and Jenny closed her eyes tiredly as the door clicked shut. Why, she wondered, when she should be relieved at the prospect of returning home, did she feel so miserable instead?

Chapter Four

"You look beautiful," the Old One purred approvingly. She bent forward, balancing on her ebony canes so she could grasp a handful of the heavily embossed material and admire it.

"Don't you think the skirts are too full? I feel like a bell," Jenny complained. She held out the weighted skirts of the cream-colored wedding gown, wondering how English women like Sarah had ever managed to put up with such discomfort on a daily basis. Layered over three stiff, floor-sweeping petticoats, the dress was tightly laced at the back and plunged daringly in the front to expose the tops of Jenny's ivory breasts. Jenny felt as though she had been squeezed into an upside-down ice-cream cone.

"Nonsense," the Old One said with a huff. "You look like a beautiful young woman . . . one who's finally come to her senses."

Her complaint would be ignored, Jenny realized. How she felt was of no consequence. It was how she looked—in front of her relatives and those of her new husband—that would matter next Saturday.

"And now for the other," the Old One said happily. She glanced at the maid. The woman bowed, her broad grin widening still further, and held out a garment of glowing red satin. "No, you stupid thing," the Old One said querulously. "Help Jenny get out of the other dress first."

Both dresses were needed—it had become customary over the years for a double wedding ceremony to take place among well-to-do Chinese families. One was traditional and the other modern, but the Old One had ensured that even the latter would retain a hint of the East. And, over the frantic protests of Jenny's mother, the Old One had stubbornly insisted that the traditional ceremony take place first.

Jenny smoothed her hands over the elegant wedding gown. It had been custom-made from a nearly priceless bolt of satin that her great-grandmother had been hoarding for years. Jenny thought uneasily of the equally valuable bolt of silk velvet that her great-grandmother was also saving for a special occasion. She knew the material was in the Old One's trunk, awaiting the birth of her first great-great-grandson. It would be used to make him a set of clothes to celebrate his first New Year's.

The maid carefully deposited the red wedding dress on the bed and rushed to undo the lacing at Jenny's back. Jenny sighed with relief as the pressure eased. The pointed stays had been digging uncomfortably into her breasts, and she had been unable to take more than a shallow breath for fifteen long minutes.

"It'll be like being married twice," Jenny mused. "Oh, thank goodness." She groaned, stepping from the undone dress. It sank gracefully to the floor, looking to Jenny like a woman curtseying. A woman curtseying in pain, she amended, taking the deepest gulp of air she could manage. She massaged her tender ribs. "That has to be the most uncomfortable dress ever made," she proclaimed.

The maid helped her don the second exquisite costume, her hands briskly moving to fasten a row of tiny silk balls and matching loops that stretched from the underarm of the dress to Jenny's knee. By the time the maid had finished, Jenny realized she had spoken too soon. The second dress was as uncomfortable as the first, but in a totally different way. This one pinioned her breasts into jutting cones and pulled tightly at her hips. *I feel like a Chinese Barbie doll,* Jenny thought with dismay. She took a tentative step forward and almost crashed to the floor.

The Old One laughed at Jenny's startled expression. "You're dressed like a goddess, but you move like an ox. Not like that—like this."

Her great-grandmother moved forward on her canes, and Jenny noticed for the first time that her gait was not only kept in check by the miniature size of her feet, but was also deliberately restrained. Watching her, Jenny shuffled obligingly forward. The tightness of the dress reminded her at every step to keep her steps small.

It reminded her of a game she had played as a child. One girl would call on the others to take a giant step forward or two baby steps forward, as the whim moved her, until the finish line was reached. Jenny discovered that by twitching her hips from side to side and taking the tiniest of steps, she could fake what her great-grandmother seemed to manage naturally.

"But how do I sit down?" she ventured.

"In that dress?" her great-grandmother asked unbelievingly. "Very carefully. Usually you stand."

Jenny looked at her, shocked. "In the old days . . . Great-grandmother, did you wear dresses like this?"

"Yes, child."

"And how did you sit down?"

"I didn't sit, Jenny. I stood. Sometimes until my feet bled."

A sudden rush of pity overtook Jenny. "How could

anyone be so cruel? Didn't my great-grandfather love you?''

Her great-grandmother looked up quickly at Jenny's troubled face. ''He honored me, Jenny. He was a good man.''

''But your feet—''

''No, Jenny.'' The Old One spoke fiercely. ''He was not a man who demanded his wife's feet be golden lilies. It was my *amah*—your great-great-great-grandmother—who caused my feet to be bound.''

''But why?''

The Old One sighed heavily. ''How can I explain a thousand-year-old tradition to a child like you? It was years before the war . . . but the times were already troubled ones in China. We fled to Hong Kong because we were merchants, and all our family wanted was to be able to do its business in peace. But we waited too long to leave . . . when we did flee, it was a hasty affair. Nearly all of our possessions were left behind. We had very little money.''

''What's that got to do with your feet?''

''I brought trouble on myself,'' the Old One said heavily. ''My sister and I . . . we were not allowed out on the streets—not even with a chaperone after we were thirteen. It seemed a foolish rule, and I was young. I wanted to see Victoria Harbor again. One day I escaped the family compound and I went for a walk. I was punished when I returned, but a whipping turned out to be the least of my worries. A man had seen me. His family offered a large *li-chin*, but on one condition."

"That your feet be bound," Jenny said softly.

"It wasn't common anymore. Especially not in Hong Kong, where it was against the law. But the Leungs were new arrivals from the mainland, rich landowners from a northern province, where women with feet as beautiful as a curved bow"—the Old One spat the words derisively—"were still desired."

Who were the Leungs? Jenny wondered. She felt unsettled by her great-grandmother's tale. She had always assumed her family's comfortable life had gone on forever—first in Hong Kong and then in Vancouver. What else was there about her family that she didn't know?

"Leung-Che was my first husband," her great-grandmother said, noting her puzzlement. "Not your great-grandfather—he was an American missionary who had the kindness to marry me after my husband died of yellow fever."

"How old were you, Great-grandmother?"

"I was twenty-six when he died." She looked fiercely at Jenny. "The first thing *your* great-grandfather did was to unbind my feet. A thousand years of tradition meant nothing to him. That is what I mean by honor. He honored me, though it was too late for my feet to be normal. And I honored him—I would have stood at his table for days if he had requested it. Do you understand, Jenny? Honor is the most important thing there is.''

Jenny, under the relentless scrutiny of her great-grandmother's eyes, gulped and nodded. She had always wondered how her feet had come to be bound. As a child, the Old One had always turned her curious inquiries aside. She hadn't dared ask the question for years. And now that she knew, she felt horrified. *Compared to that, what do I have to complain about?* she thought suddenly.

Her great-grandmother lifted her chin. ''And now because I can sit, I will sit,'' she said regally. The maid rushed to bring her a chair. ''Now turn—turn, Jenny, so I can see what a beautiful bride you will make.''

Jenny, still disturbed by her great-grandmother's revelation, spun obediently. Her great-grandmother, her chin held imperially high, watched from her wicker chair like visiting royalty. The sleeveless dress brought Jenny's hair into vivid contrast, and her dark eyes stood out starkly against its rich color. With its tight body, winged mandarin collar, and body-clinging length, the dress lent Jenny the sophistication of a much older woman.

''*Ei yah,*'' the Old One said, fanning herself gently. ''You look like every man's desire in that dress. Your skin shines like alabaster.''

Jenny's complexion paled still more. Every man's desire but one, she thought unhappily. What would he think of this dress? Red—the color of happiness, of passion, of blood—hers to mix with Edward Li's to produce the next generation. It was every color, Jenny thought, every color except the color of love.

"Grandmother, why do I have to marry at all? Why can't I just stay here with you?"

The Old One stared down at her feet. "I asked my *amah* the same question once," she said at last. "I can only tell you what she told me. It is your duty to marry."

She fell silent, and Jenny wondered if she were thinking of the bolt of silk velvet. "Lots of women don't marry, Great-grandmother," Jenny prompted.

"There is no happiness in this world for a woman whose womb remains barren," her great-grandmother retorted.

Yes, she had been thinking of children, Jenny thought with annoyance. "I want children," she said aloud. She took a deep breath and plunged on. "But I don't love Edward—and I don't think he loves me, either."

There, she had finally said it. She waited, somewhat fearfully, for her tiny great-grandmother to explode.

Instead of launching into a tirade, the Old One turned her head to stare out the window. Her eyes admired the Japanese plum tree. It was fifteen years old and only now, after many seasons, finally ready to

produce fruit. She stared silently at the ripening pur-
plish plums, and Jenny dared another question.

"Did you have any children with your first
husband?"

The Old One started. "No," she said shortly. Jenny
wondered at the fleeting smile that darted across her
great-grandmother's face.

"What about love?" she demanded. She thought of
Lukas and pushed the thought away, dismissing it as
unworthy. "How can I marry without love?"

"What fire," the Old One said quizzically, regard-
ing her great-grandchild. "But you have no sense of
duty." She rapped with one cane at her tiny feet. "My
amah loved me. My feet were bound out of love. It
wasn't just the *li-chin*—the bride-price. My mother
believed it was my best chance for a prosperous marriage. Ah! How I cried! Every night she would unwrap
the binding cloths, only to wind fresh ones even more
tightly around my aching feet. Afterward, I would go
out to the garden and swing my feet to and fro to ease
the pain. That was love, Jenny. Love often hurts."

Jenny's eyes suddenly filled with tears at the
thought of her suffering. *I promise, Great-
grandmother. . . .* "I'm an ungrateful girl," she said
aloud. She straightened suddenly and bowed, speaking
formally. "If you could bear that from a sense of duty,
honored Great-grandmother, then I must do this little
thing to please you."

The Old One smiled warmly. But Jenny, nevertheless, felt the bonds of her promise tighten like a vise around her heart. For her, as for her great-grandmother, she knew the pain would never cease.

Shouts of excitement filtered up from the hall below, and the Old One called sharply to the maid. She bowed and left the bedroom, returning moments later with a broad grin on her good-natured face.

''The pig has arrived,'' she announced grandly.

The room was instantly plunged into a flurry of excitement. ''Help me up, help me up,'' the Old One demanded as she struggled to her feet. ''No—help Jenny, help Jenny.'' But Jenny's fingers were already flying down the closure of her dress, and the maid returned to help the Old One with her canes.

Jenny carelessly threw the dress on the bed and struggled into an ordinary one. She ran a brush through her hair and then hurried after her great-grandmother, who was rushing to reach the top of the stairs as quickly as she could. A crowd of smiling servants had gathered there to gawk at the sight below. They parted politely to allow the women to descend.

Below, Edward Li, perspiring profusely, was almost obscured under the largest pig Jenny had ever seen. The enormous head lolled lifelessly forward on his right shoulder. One hairy jowl was snuggled up against his cheek. The carcass had made a ruinous mess of his conservative suit. Jenny studied Edward's trembling legs with interest. *Maybe he'll fall,* she thought heartlessly.

It was a time-honored custom that the bridegroom's family bring presents of food in increasing extravagance to the home of his intended bride. The pig was the last and the most important, a task entrusted only to the prospective bridegroom. The larger the pig, the greater the prestige, Jenny knew. But ironclad custom dictated that no one was allowed to help the groom carry it. Edward had taken on more of an ordeal than he had expected, she thought with satisfaction—and to drop the pig would mean hideously bad luck.

"I bring . . . this poor . . . token . . . of my appreciation," he said between grunts and gasps.

It's too much for him, Jenny thought with delight. *Does that mean bad luck for both of us or just for him?* As she had expected, Edward's thin legs buckled. Two of the servants rushed forward to relieve him of his burden. Before they could reach him, he dropped it. A maid hurriedly brought a sheet, spreading it out on the marble floor, and the servants clumsily rolled the pig onto it.

Edward bowed shakily and backed out of the open front door. He was trailed by members of his own beaming family, who clapped him gingerly on the back of his ruined suit and congratulated him on the size of the pig. *They act like he didn't drop it,* Jenny thought. The door was scarcely shut on their departing backs when she laughed aloud.

"How rude," her father said sharply. "Have you no respect?" His spectacled eyes glittered.

Crestfallen, Jenny ducked her head. "I'm sorry, Father . . . it's just that Edward looked so funny."

"Funny." He snorted. "That was the largest pig I have ever seen." To Jenny's amazement, he burst into laughter. The mood was infectious. Edward, for all his mammoth undertaking, had looked absurd. Soon everyone was convulsed. Even the servants were smiling.

Ben came into the foyer from the back entrance and stopped. He stared at them as if they had gone mad. "What's so funny?" he asked. "And what's that pig doing on the floor?" His voice scaled up in horror as he regarded the hulking carcass.

That set them off again into another gale of uncontrollable mirth. Between gasps, Jenny managed to explain the joke, and at last Ben began to smile too. He drew her aside, still laughing, glancing sideways at their parents and the Old One.

"Jenny, I have to talk to you about something."

"Well, tell me," she said, her eyes filled with mirth.

"Not here," he said quickly. "We have to go out." He turned to his great-grandmother. "Old One," he asked formally, "can I take Jenny out for a while?"

"There's some hair combs I want to buy," Jenny

improvised hastily, backing up her brother. "Then I can do my hair in a traditional style for the wedding," she added wheedlingly.

Her great-grandmother beamed. "Very well," she said. "But you"—she pointed sternly at Ben—"make sure you bring her back in an hour. We've still got another dress fitting before we're finished."

"I will, Old One."

Still smiling at the memory of Edward and his pig, the Old One tottered away in the direction of the kitchen. Once there, she would fussily inspect the progress made by the army of pastry chefs hired to make special rice cakes and pastries for the wedding.

"Let's go to the park," her brother suggested after the Old One was out of earshot.

"Great," Jenny said with a grumble. "I seem to do nothing these days but change clothes." Nevertheless, she returned upstairs and reappeared minutes later in a pair of leggy jeans and a striped sweatshirt.

As they sped past the luxury homes on Marine Drive, Jenny wondered what Ben wanted to talk about. "So tell me."

"No. Not here."

"Fine." She stretched like a cat, feeling stiff from all the dress fittings. Her role as bride had so far consisted of standing still. Would that also be her fate once she was married? Jenny tried to dispel the gloomy thought by pushing the button to open her window. She put her face out the window, enjoying the sensation of the air rushing by.

"Don't do that," Ben said irritably. "It wrecks the air-conditioning."

Jenny gave him a dirty look and shut the window. "I never knew getting ready for a wedding could be so time-consuming," she complained. "I've barely managed to keep up with the deadline for my book."

She waited expectantly, but Ben didn't ask her whether she was finished. What was eating him? she wondered. *Maybe he's mad I made him go get my manuscript from the apartment,* she thought suddenly. *But that wouldn't be like Ben,* she realized. *He knows how much I depend on him.*

With a guilty start, she suddenly remembered that she hadn't told the landlady she wouldn't be returning. But the damage deposit should more than make up for the few days the apartment was likely to be empty, she rationalized. She could just mail the key back to her with a note.

The car lurched around the curve of the off-ramp as they left the bridge, and Jenny winced. "Slow down, Ben."

"Sure," he said distantly. "Why not?" But his speed crept up again—it was like Ben was in another world, Jenny thought worriedly—and by the time they reached the entrance of the park, she was forced to remind him to slow down again.

Ben looked at her expressionlessly and spun the car into the graveled parking lot opposite the seawall. She gave him a speculative look and then got out of the car, slamming the door. Ordinarily, Ben would have screeched at such disrespect to his most prized possession. But he was silent, alerting Jenny to the fact that something was very wrong indeed.

Two joggers in sun hats and cutoff jeans padded past the seawall. Jenny looked out at Burrard Inlet, staring at the whitecaps foaming at the tips of the waves. Seagulls were wheeling and crying overhead like airborne cats. The blocky forms of garbage scows could be seen in the distance. She crossed the road to sit down on the rock ledge and patted it, enjoying the feel of the damp moss springing up to greet her hand. Ben slouched down beside her. He dangled his legs over the ledge and began banging his heels on the granite blocks.

"Jenny, Lukas is in trouble," he said quietly.

Jenny's heart gave an uneasy leap. A tide of complicated emotions washed over her. "Why should I care?" she asked scornfully.

Ben's normally cheerful face grew somber. "Look, Jenny . . . this isn't easy to explain. You haven't been around these people—the nightlife—the way I have. I don't know that Lukas is a gang member . . . and I don't know that he isn't."

"What do you mean?" she asked urgently.

Ben lowered his voice as a flock of lunch-hour joggers—grown as numerous as the seagulls with the sun now directly overhead—loped by. "The word is that Lukas is a narc—an undercover cop. If he is, he's a darn good one. He's worked his way into a really scary set of people."

Jenny was stunned. *Not a gang member!* A ray of hope rose up, threatening to overwhelm all of her carefully considered reasons for marrying Edward. The bonds holding her heart chafed uncomfortably. She suddenly remembered that Lukas had seemed curiously relieved when she told him she didn't think he was a criminal.

If he was a policeman that would certainly explain it, she thought excitedly.

Her mind churned, exhuming every scrap she could remember about Lukas. But what about that package? Maybe it was something else, she thought, her heart beating wildly. Could Lukas have been passing information, not drugs? She thought of the girl she had met in the washroom and shivered with distaste. Samantha—she remembered her name now—had said she used to work for Rocky. But if Lukas was a narc . . .

She turned suddenly to Ben, her eyes wide. "But if people suspect he's a narc, isn't he in danger?"

Her brother looked at her unhappily. "That's really what I wanted to talk to you about. I overheard something and I'm trying to decide if I should go to the police.''

Jenny clambered off the wall and sat down on the thick carpet of grass. She pulled her knees up to her chin and rocked slowly back and forth, trying to absorb her brother's words.

Ben swung his legs back over the wall and slid down beside her. ''When you're working a gig, the club people seem to forget about you when you're not playing. They get used to you being around—it's like you're a fixture, not somebody with ears and eyes. I've heard all kinds of things. But what I heard today was the worst. There's a big deal going down tonight. One of the bouncers at the club was talking about it on the phone. The other band members say he's hooked into the Vancouver crime scene in a big way.''

''And—?''

Ben shook his head, impatient with his own inability to get to the point. ''Anyway, there's an illegal shipment coming in on an oil tanker,'' he said rapidly. ''Lukas is going to be there to help make the deal. But what he doesn't know is that they suspect him. They're going to kidnap him and take him back to Hong Kong . . . then they'll plant some drugs on him and report him to the authorities.''

''But they execute drug dealers there!''

''They're counting on that,'' Ben said grimly. ''There's worse—they're going to blind him and cut out his tongue so he can't tell anyone if he is a cop. The authorities will just think he came out the worst in a drug squabble.''

Jenny straightened with horror. "Oh, Ben," she whispered. "You have to go to the police."

"That's where it gets tricky," he said weakly. "If I go to the police I'm dead meat." His eyes stared into Jenny's, begging her to understand. "The bouncer *knows* I overheard him. I tried to duck back into the dressing room before he was off the phone, but he saw me. Jenny . . . you should have seen the way he looked at me. If anything happens to their deal, I'm a dead man."

"What about police protection?" Jenny said eagerly. "What about those witness-protection programs they have?"

Her brother gave her an ironic look. "I could build one hell of a rock career that way, couldn't I? Maybe call myself the Invisible Man. That ought to sell millions of compact discs. Look, Jenny . . . it's up to you. If you think I should go to the police, I will."

Ben got up abruptly and began walking away.

"Ben—?"

"I'll be right back," he said. "I need some space to think things over."

Jenny dropped her head to her knees for a moment and cradled it in her arms. She looked up to stare dejectedly at her brother's retreating form. What a terrible choice he had presented her with—she couldn't endanger her own brother. But could she sacrifice Lukas?

Since we were children, this has always been Ben's way, she thought angrily. *Whenever he gets himself into a jam he comes to me, thinking his big sister can straighten it out for him. It isn't fair!*

Jenny ground her closed fist into the tightly woven grass. What could she do? Common sense told her they should go to the police. But police protection? It just wouldn't be good enough for Ben—especially now, with the Snow Tigers on the brink of success. If Ben had to give up playing publicly, it would kill him. Not physically, maybe. But Jenny knew Ben would be a hollow shell, with nothing really alive inside, if he had to give up his music.

But what about Lukas? With Ben's revelation, the careful barriers she had erected against him had melted as easily as summer hail. The memories sprang forward, as raw and as painful as a reopened wound. Jenny felt the urgent press of his lips once more and the strong clasp of his hand atop hers. Her thoughts flew to the smoldering lights of his amber eyes and the way he had looked at her on the junk. Shaken in its assumption that Lukas was a criminal, her mind had once again been overtaken by her heart.

* * *

There was something she could do for him, Sarah *realized suddenly. She surveyed the neglected drawing room and a twinkle came into her eyes.*

She begged a serviceable apron and broom from a cook in the kitchens and set to work, discovering what appeared to be the accumulated dirt of a decade. Why, I fancy he hasn't allowed this room to be cleaned since his wife died, *Sarah thought indignantly. Her sharp eyes spotted a mound of slut's wool under the spindly legs of the virginal. She attacked it with the broom, sneezing vigorously as a cloud of dust billowed up to surround her.*

A powerful arm circled her ribs and snapped her back, cutting off her wind in midsneeze. Sarah gasped for air and stumbled as she was suddenly released. She coughed convulsively. Sir Randolph, his hands astride his hips, was still in riding attire, she saw when she had caught her breath. His face was red with rage.

"You infernal woman! The household has been turned upside down since you arrived! How dare you defy my orders when I specifically gave you instructions that the drawing room was to be left as it is."

Panting, Sarah tossed her head angrily. "Your lordship, there's no virginal in the schoolroom," she improvised. "How can I give the children their music lessons in this chaos? Don't you care enough about them to see that they have a proper education?"

"Do you always take it upon yourself to disobey

your master's instructions? I said the room was not to be cleaned, and what I say, I mean." He viciously struck at the virginal with his riding crop, and the ivory keys chimed in protest.

Alarmed, Sarah shrank back. Then she straightened. No, she wouldn't . . . she absolutely refused to give in to his ridiculous temper. "Is your lordship always so certain that he's right?" she challenged.

What would Sarah do in a situation like this? Jenny wondered. She'd take the bull by the horns, she decided firmly, and wrenched her mind away to concentrate on the problem at hand.

Jenny stretched out and rolled over on her stomach. She thought furiously, uprooting the grass into neat little piles. Everyone kept telling her she was so naive, so inexperienced . . . maybe for once she could turn that to her advantage.

Struck by the beginning of an idea, she formed one of the grass piles into a rectangle. That was the oil tanker. She sprinkled a long line of torn grass from it to another pile. And there was the apartment.

Her brother returned five minutes later, looking, if anything, even more miserable. "I'm sorry, Jenny. I had no business trying to stick you with the decision. I've decided myself—I'm going to go to the police." He sank down on the grass and stared up at the sky. "What are you doing?" he asked listlessly.

"Conducting a dress rehearsal. You won't have to go to the police, Ben—I've got an idea," she said excitedly. Her eyes glowed. "Do you think you could stand to loan me your car?"

Chapter Five

The moon was full, casting a bright radiance on the dockyards ahead. Jenny felt a thrill of nervous anticipation wash over her. She parked the Ferrari and silently got out. She hesitated, listening for a moment to the wind jangling the riggings of the moored ships. Gathering her nerve, she threw back her shoulders and walked boldly out into the revealing moonlight. Inside, she couldn't help feeling as conspicuous as the last dress on a sales rack.

As she walked down the pier, she peered closely at the paint-blistered names and numbers of each ship. Perhaps she should have brought Ben, she thought worriedly. She didn't know North Vancouver very well, and Ben worked down here every day. No—

there was no way she could have brought him, she reminded herself. If she had brought Ben he would have refused to leave her here alone.

Jenny's eyes seized with relief on a distant row of lettering. There it was—just as her brother had told her. The *Orient Rose* looked abandoned; its rusted body screamed out for a coat of paint. As Jenny strode closer, she heard voices. Her courage suddenly failed her and she moved quickly to duck behind a helter-skelter pile of pallets before the three men at the foot of the gangway could turn and see her. A breeze sent the long ends of her blue scarf flying past the concealing bulk of the pallets. Feeling as if she were reeling in a kite, she hastily hauled the escaping scarf back and tucked it out of sight.

"How long do we have to hang around here?" a voice said clearly. Her heart thrilled with recognition. She edged closer.

"It shouldn't be more than an hour," another male voice said. Jenny shivered with distaste at its drawling tone. She looked carefully through the slots of the wooden pallets, taking advantage of a warped board that allowed her a clear, if somewhat restricted, view.

She saw that the man standing next to Rocky was Chinese and dressed in a business suit that shone out palely against the rusting hulk. But Jenny had eyes only for the third man. Wearing a black leather jacket, Lukas looked dangerous. As dangerous as Rocky, she realized with a sinking heart. What if Ben were wrong?

I can't back out now, Jenny thought. *Lukas will be killed if I do.* She straightened and then boldly walked out from behind the pallets. "Oh, God, don't let Ben be wrong," she whispered to herself. She smoothed her clothes and mentally blessed Jin Sing for being kind enough to lend her the old uniform.

She had made quite a stir when she had arrived earlier at the restaurant. The waitresses crowded out into the street, oohing and aahing. Jin Sing's eyes traveled unbelievingly over Ben's immaculate Ferrari.

Glenda turned a nasty shade of pink when she saw the car. "I could have one of those if I wanted," she said. "I've got friends who'll do anything I ask."

"Shut up," Jin Sing said. "You miss another shift and those creeps will be all you do have."

Jenny ignored Glenda's furious sputter and turned pleading eyes on Jin Sing. "Why do you want a uniform?" the old cook asked, his eyes troubled.

Jenny was about to tell him a lie, but stopped. "Because I need it," she said flatly. Jin Sing took another look at her desperate face and visibly weakened.

"Are you mixed up in something illegal?" His eyes moved again to study the expensive vehicle. "That gangster was asking about you."

Rocky? Jenny had thought. Or was it Lukas? She didn't dare ask. If she had, Jenny thought now, the whole story would have spilled out. It had been hard enough to convince her brother. She didn't want to take the chance of Jin Sing putting a stop to her plans.

"I can't tell you what it's for," she said desperately, "but what I'm doing is not illegal. I'm trying to save someone's life."

Jin Sing lent her the uniform—reluctantly—but he refused to take any money for it.

"Make sure you return it," he ordered her. Then his eyes softened. "I want to know that you're safe."

Jin Sing had been wonderful, but safe was not something she was feeling at the moment, Jenny thought as she drew closer to the oil tanker. Rocky, who was the farthest from the gangway, turned to flip a cigarette butt into the greasy water lapping against the pier. His eyes narrowed when he saw her and then widened in recognition.

"It's the little waitress—babe, what you doing down here? Ain't you got a teapot to mind?" He chuckled throatily.

Jenny couldn't help herself. Her hands dropped to her skirt and yanked its short length down to cover more of her legs.

At Rocky's words, the man in the suit instantly put his right hand inside his jacket. Jenny gulped and kept on going. Her legs felt like wooden stilts. She walked right up to Lukas and looked inquiringly at him. But after his first start of recognition, the amber eyes that she remembered so well had gone flat and unreadable.

"Well," she said, trembling, "how about it? How come you forgot our date again?" She glared at him as haughtily as she could manage. She pulled her coat together, both to ward off Rocky's unwelcome scrutiny and to hide the knocking of her knees.

Rocky hooted. "Hey, Lukas . . . you been making time with my girl?"

Lukas didn't answer. His eyes flashed at Jenny like twin warning lights. She lifted her chin imperiously and didn't budge.

"Push off now, babe," Rocky said, growing tired of the exchange. "We got things going on."

"No," Jenny said. Her voice trembled and then firmed into a whine. "Lukas, you promised. You said you wouldn't forget again."

Her eyes looked beseechingly into his fixed gaze, willing him to catch on. *Come on, come on,* she thought. The silent seconds dragged on.

"Look, I'm sorry I forgot," he said suddenly. "I'll take you back to the restaurant." He took her arm and Jenny almost fainted with relief.

The Chinese man whispered sharply to Rocky. "Not so fast," Rocky said. "We got business—remember?" He stepped forward and his companion moved up close behind him.

"Look," Lukas said reasonably—he pulled Jenny

closer—"you said it would be an hour." He winked. "I can do a lot in an hour."

Jenny held her breath. For a moment, Rocky's stance remained threatening. Then he relaxed. "Yeah, well," he said with a chuckle. His eyes swept over Jenny's figure. "I guess. But hurry it up, will you?" He moved abruptly aside.

Jenny's legs refused to move. Lukas strengthened his grip on her hand and tugged impatiently. Her legs unthawed at last, and they walked slowly away.

They turned the corner of the first warehouse at the edge of the shipyard, and Jenny turned thankfully to Lukas. He grabbed her by the shoulders, spinning her flat against the rough bricks. Jenny felt the air go out of her with a *whoosh!*

"Now what was that all about?" he said harshly. "And it had better be good."

"I can't tell you here." Jenny gasped. She twisted away from his hands. "Let's go back to . . . my apartment."

She could get the car later, she decided. It was too close to the docks to safely start up. The last thing she wanted to do was attract the attention of Rocky or the other man.

They walked quickly, silently, and reached the apartment building in fifteen minutes. How familiar it all was, Jenny thought. She darted a quick look around the neighborhood, smiling sentimentally at the sight of the flapping billboard. *It seems so long ago already,* she thought.

They entered the building quietly, but the landlady scurried out before they could mount the first landing. Her suspicious eyes peered out from beneath a torn scarf fixed to hold an irregular line of curlers in place. She hovered cautiously in the doorway of her dark apartment, ready to retreat at the first sign of danger. Jenny saw a look of recognition dawn on her thin features, and her mouth shrank into an accusing circle. "You're a week behind. I thought you'd skipped."

Coloring, Jenny assured her that she hadn't. She searched for her wallet and paid her the two hundred on the spot. Lukas's face darkened with disapproval. Jenny looked at him quickly. *He's wondering where I got the money,* she thought, feeling embarrassed. *But I can explain that now. And I can tell him who Ben is.* Jenny refused to consider other things—like her engagement to Edward—that might be more difficult to explain.

Satisfied, the old woman shuffled back to bed. They mounted the stairs and Jenny became very aware of the lithe form bumping against her own on the narrow steps. Her heart began to pound. At last they were in the apartment. Lukas turned on the lights, and Jenny locked the door, feeling weak with relief. She had actually managed to pull it off! Shaking, she sat down on the worn couch and took off her coat.

Lukas was looking at her curiously. "The last time I saw you, you spit on my feet."

"That was different," Jenny said haltingly. She reddened. "Listen, there's no time to waste."

As Jenny explained, telling him about the conversation her brother had overhead, she was surprised to see a look of relief, not alarm, on his face.

". . . and they were going to turn you loose with some drugs and tell the police. They would have hung you, Lukas."

Again his expression was not what Jenny expected. He looked angry. "You idiot," he said roughly, "you could have gotten yourself killed."

Jenny felt angry. How dare he? Was that how he saw it? She had just saved his life and he was mad at her. "Does Rocky know where I live?" she asked abruptly. "Did you tell him?"

"Of course not," he said quickly.

"Then there's your excuse. They'll think you were . . . otherwise involved and forgot to come back." She blushed. "That way my brother's off the hook and you're free to go about your business."

"You must love your brother very much to go this kind of trouble," Lukas said slowly. "Don't you realize what Rocky and that other man are? How much danger you were in?"

For the second time since Jenny had known him, his manner took on a kind of watchfulness. She felt strongly that much depended on her answer. But Jenny, angry at his ungratefulness, didn't care. ''I do love my brother very much,'' she said coldly. ''Good-bye.''

She threw the keys in the direction of the desk and rose. ''If you stay here for a while they won't suspect a thing.'' She marched to the door. Lukas sprang to block her. She was surprised at how quickly he could move.

''Not so fast. Someone might see you alone and tell Rocky. I think he'd be suspicious, don't you?'' His eyes flared, and Jenny felt herself being pressed against the wall. ''I think that if you're going to tell a whopper like that, then you should have the guts to carry it through,'' he whispered. His hands reached up, and Jenny felt the thin scarf sliding from her neck.

She strained to get away from him. He bent forward, his massive shoulders blocking out the light, and Jenny opened her mouth to protest. As she pushed forward, his lips met hers. They numbed her with a violent kiss that drained her of all anger. His hands rose to her shoulders, massaging them, forcing her whole body into the embrace. Jenny sighed as his hands dropped to her waist.

His grip tightened, and Jenny was suddenly, bewilderingly, in midair. Lukas could move as quickly as a big cat, she realized in consternation.

Kisses rained on her upturned face. He gently lowered her back to the floor, but kept firm hold of her waist, sending shivers of delight coursing through her. Jenny pulled herself away and ran her hands over his smoothly muscled arms, seeking to penetrate the fabric to the man beneath.

Oh, God,'' he said. "Don't you ever spit on me again.''

Jenny laughed, feeling half hysterical. Lukas plunged his hands into her hair, bringing her lips to his in a passionate kiss that she eagerly met halfway. He pulled back without warning and stared searchingly at her until Jenny grew uncomfortable and edged away.

"I asked about you," he said finally. "That old cook didn't want to talk much, but he finally told me that you had quit—that your family had arrived early. That wasn't true, was it? Your English is too perfect. You've lived here all along, haven't you?"

Jenny's heart faltered in midbeat. "I . . . I had my reasons for telling you that," she said. Her face grew unhappy, and Lukas moved closer. He raised one hand to stroke the delicate slant of her cheek. His gentle touch reminded her of her great-grandmother's, and Jenny's eyes suddenly brimmed with tears.

Had she lost her mind? She was to marry in six short days. It was her duty to obey her great-grandmother and marry Edward. She had promised . . . promised. Jenny lowered her head. She pulled away from Lukas's touch, though every square inch of her body was begging her to stay. She forced herself to move to the door. She heard the couch creak as Lukas sat down, and she looked quickly at him. His commanding eyebrows had drawn together in a stormy line.

"Where are you going?"

Jenny turned her head away, blinking back tears. It was her duty to obey. It was a matter of honor. But she knew now that what she felt for Lukas was something special. "I must go," she said abruptly. She picked up her scarf and her coat.

"Let me come with you," Lukas urged.

"No. I'll be all right. I have my brother's car."

"When will I see you again?"

"I can't see you," Jenny said woodenly. Her next words came out in a desperate rush. "I am to be married." How her heart froze at the sound of those words!

Lukas got up. "Do you love him?"

Jenny lowered her head and said nothing.

"You do love him," he said savagely. His eyes grew cold, and he turned to the window. *He looks like a tiger,* Jenny thought unhappily. *A tiger intent on more rewarding prey.*

He stared down at the street. "It seems safe enough," he said, his words flat. "You should get going."

Each word left a claw mark on Jenny's heart. She fled, stumbling on the worn carpet of the stairs. She wanted to tell him—that it was him she loved, not Edward. But how could she? Her destiny was as irrevocably fixed as the stars. She would marry Edward.

She wandered the empty streets back to the car in a daze. Lukas must despise her, she thought unhappily. Twice she had led him on, unable to fight the insistent need that gripped her whenever she was with him.

When she reached the Ferrari, she stared, somewhat bitterly, at its color. Aglow in the moonlight, it shone as brightly as the first wedding dress she had tried on that morning. She got in, trembling at the tumult of colliding emotions in her heart. *Will I ever be able to forget him?*

A bulky form materialized next to the car, and she felt joy exploding in her heart. Lukas must have followed her, she thought. And then her face froze with horror as a second man appeared.

"Glenda was right," Rocky said to his Chinese companion. "It is a nice car."

At first, the Old One's eyes widened in astonishment at the size of the man brought to her by her great-grandson. Then they narrowed, busily measuring his bulk against her own diminutive proportions.

Would this be the fate of the next generation? she thought worriedly. Her mind flashed to the waiting bolt of silk velvet in her trunk. She was suddenly horrified. *Why, there might not be enough!*

"Were you born here?" she asked quickly.

"Yes, Respected One. I was."

At least he has manners, the Old One thought grudgingly. With her worst fears confirmed, she fell silent, worriedly turning the problem over in her mind. Would a strictly Chinese diet keep a pregnant woman from producing a giant? she wondered.

Lukas studied her in turn, wholly aware that the tiny woman before him would be the dominant power in Jenny's life. Beside him, Jenny's brother stifled a yawn. No one was getting any sleep this night, but Lukas saw that the old woman, at least, looked wide awake and alert. His heart turned over with pity and revulsion as he caught sight of her feet. It was little wonder she had such an appalling lack of concern for Jenny's happiness, he thought harshly. Her own life had been crippled since childhood.

His eyes flickered dangerously to the fussily dressed man standing behind her chair. Edward Li had the eyes of a money changer, as his mother used to say. What a husband for Jenny! The memory of her slim form rose up to haunt him, and he grew impatient. What was the old woman hesitating for? Didn't they realize Jenny was in danger?

Still concerned with eugenics, the Old One pressed on. "Are all your family so large? I've heard tell they put some chemical in the drinking water of this new land.''

Startled, Lukas threw back his head and laughed aloud. ''No, Respected One. It's not the water. I am Hanh. The men of my family have always been large.''

The Old One nodded, both relieved and—against her will—impressed. The Hanhs were of a lineage superior to her own. Mixing with the Mongols over the centuries, they had risen to the position of imperial guards to the Mandarins. Fierce warriors, their numbers had been decimated during the revolution. Some, she remembered, had escaped to Hong Kong, taking refuge under the British rule.

She sighed to herself, thinking of Jenny. Her great-granddaughter thought of them as ancient times, she knew. The innocence of the young colored the past as a distant event that had no bearing on their own untarnished future. It was better that way, the Old One thought, regretting that she had told her great-granddaughter the story of her feet. She shifted uneasily in her chair.

She hadn't told Jenny how, for the duration of her first marriage, she had denied her husband children. He had beaten her and called her barren. But he had refused to let her return to her family as she had hoped he would. If Leung-Che had known about the potions she obtained from an herbalist sworn to secrecy, he would have killed her. It was a woman's revenge: complete and implacable. None of Leung-Che's seed had survived to walk the earth.

She stared now at this new threat to her security. *What threatens Jenny threatens me,* she thought angrily. "You are a policeman," she said aloud.

Like nearly all Chinese of her generation, the Old One associated policemen with soldiers. She considered both to be at the bottom of the heap. Even now, few Chinese families wanted even their youngest son to become a policeman. With so few policemen knowledgeable in the language, they were highly sought after, she knew. *But who could blame their families for not wanting their children to become involved?* the Old One thought. Everyone wanted the best thing for their children. "A policeman," she repeated with distaste.

"What I am is my business," Lukas said firmly.

Ben gave him a look of surprise. When Lukas had come seeking him at the club, he had flashed a policeman's identification at him. And learning of Jenny's failure to return home, he had instantly phoned a specialized surveillance unit to search for the missing car. *Can't he say anything straight out?* Ben wondered. No wonder he was driving Jenny nuts.

"Then what are you? A criminal?" The Old One's anger deepened. "If Jenny is not with you, then where is she?"

"I do not know, Respected One. Like you, I had hoped to find her home by now." Lukas suddenly leaned forward. "If Jenny is not with you, then where is she?" he challenged her. "Or maybe she is here, but you don't want me to see her."

The Old One's jaw dropped at the affront. "My great-granddaughter is not here," she said icily. "She has not been seen since my worthless great-grandson decided to involve her in his problems." She directed a wilting look in Ben's direction.

"She insisted," Ben protested. He looked around the sitting room, hoping to find support, but came up empty. "She was worried about me and . . . she begged me not to involve the family."

"*You* were the one who didn't want to involve the family," the Old One said. "If you had anything but music in that head of yours, you would have realized it was exactly what you should have done."

She redirected her anger to the giant stranger. Unlike Ben, who assumed with youthful arrogance that Jenny had risked herself to save only him, she saw things more clearly. "You never answered my question. Who are you? What kind of man did my great-granddaughter sacrifice herself to save?"

A wounded gasp shot out from behind her. Edward's eyes moved resentfully over the giant bulk of the stranger.

"I told you," Lukas said, his jaw tightening. "I am Hanh. My father is Hanh Shipping, and I am his son."

The Old One was thunderstruck. Edward's face lost its resentment and took on a fawning look.

She had never dreamed he meant that. Hanh Shipping was one of the largest shipping concerns on the West Coast. The young man in front of her—who she had just been insulting, she remembered uneasily— was heir to a shipping empire! That explained why he had seemed curiously unimpressed with the luxury of their home, she thought suddenly. The Hanhs could buy this house—or the whole block, for that matter— without blinking an eye.

"I have been working with the police," Lukas admitted. "But they badly needed someone to go undercover—someone Chinese."

"Why would a Hanh do that?" the Old One wondered aloud.

"Because someone is smuggling drugs on our ships," he said flatly. "My father's been threatened, and we decided it was time to fight back." His eyes glinted like daggers.

"Drugs are involved?" The Old One suddenly felt weak. "Then Jenny is in great danger." Her voice firmed, and in it, for the first time, Lukas heard her love for Jenny. "You . . . find her. We will do every-thing we can to help." The Old One struggled to rise, and Edward bent solicitously to help her up.

"I will find her, Respected One."

"You had better," the Old One snapped. She drew herself up on her canes and glared at him, a tiny wraith of a woman who had survived wars, a revolution, and twice been uprooted from her home. "Your ancestors would not fail."

Lukas stiffened at the challenge. "I'll find her," he repeated. He studied her retreating back with new respect. She had known just where to needle him. What an aggravating old woman! He smiled grimly, suddenly divining the source of Jenny's deliciously independent spirit. He wondered if Jenny knew it herself. It was a trait in her that he found excitingly different from other women he had met. It was the mark of a survivor.

Lukas talked to the family and servants. He hoped to unearth a clue that might lead him in the right direction. Privately, he continued to wonder if Jenny had rebelled for a second time and had again struck out on her own.

Jenny's great-grandmother had been as good as her word, he discovered. When he asked to see Jenny's bedroom, his request was met without demur. Ben showed him, his eyes still guilty. *He should look guilty,* Lukas thought. *How could he let her get mixed up in a harebrained scheme like that?*

Lukas fingered the pages of Jenny's manuscript and sat down to leaf through the pages. His eyebrows drew together in surprise as he read. A phone jangled, and a sleepy servant moved to answer it. Bowing politely, he gestured Lukas to the phone. Lukas spoke briefly into the receiver and listened intently. His forehead wrinkled worriedly. "It's your car," he told Ben, and replaced the receiver. "They've found it."

Ben looked momentarily pleased. "But what about Jenny?"

"Nothing," Lukas said heavily. "The car's been stripped"—he smiled at Ben's struggle to hide his dismay—"but I'll go take a look."

Lukas was growing worried, but he didn't explain why to Ben. Until the car was found, the hope still existed that Jenny had decided to strike out on her own. Now he just didn't know. He drove his used Trans Am—it had been a lark to drive the muscle car when he first went undercover six months ago, but he felt silly driving it now—to the lot off Main Street where the car had been found.

It had been stripped all right, Lukas noted. Not only its stereo system, but its fenders, tires, and doors had been removed. He was surprised no one had thought to pry the motor loose.

He leaned inside, searching painstakingly through its glove box and inside the upholstery. A flash of blue caught his eye as he pushed down on the driver's seat. He pulled at it and extracted a translucent blue scarf.

He held it to his nose, and his senses suddenly reeled with Jenny's floral perfume.

So, he thought—she did make it back to the car. Then she hadn't tried to run away again. She would never take her brother's car with her. And she certainly wouldn't abandon it here. Shaking his head with frustration, he continued his search. Nothing. Lukas lightly ran the scarf through his fingers, remembering Jenny at the apartment. The end was torn, he noticed. He remembered coaxing it from her neck . . . her skin smooth as cream . . . her eyes studying him as though she had never seen a man before. He shook his head again, this time to clear it.

She was also exasperating, he thought, remembering her impudently raised chin. But no woman had ever attracted him like this before. She was very like the girls his parents had suggested to him. And then again, she was not. He had to find her.

But after a thorough search, Lukas had discovered nothing else to connect the car to Jenny. Something nagged at him. What had Jenny said before she left the apartment? That she would be safe—that she had her brother's car. But wait . . . there were no night buses to the dock area from Chinatown, Lukas suddenly remembered. Surely she hadn't walked all the way in the dark from the apartment to rescue him. She must have driven to the docks first and parked the car there. He cursed himself again for letting her leave the apartment alone. It wasn't Ben's fault she was missing; it was his.

Lukas drove to the shipyard. He searched the parking areas with a flashlight, walking carefully in a circle that began on the outer perimeter of each until he reached its center. It was nearing dawn before he finally spied faint tracks on the ground near a fenced compound. They were scuffed as though there had been a struggle. But it could have been anything, he thought.

Discouraged, Lukas rose from his crouch and found himself faced with a bit of tattered cloth held by the wind against the mesh of the wire fence. He carefully separated the fragment from the mesh and rose to look at it. The thin cloth fluttered delicately against his hand, the size and color of a tiny blue butterfly.

Chapter Six

Sarah raised one wan hand to her blister-hot fore-head and realized she felt no better. The days and nights of nursing Sir Randolph back from the brink of death had worn her out. She felt like a pale wraith of her former self.

She picked up the clean basin with an effort. Catching hold of the oaken rail with one hand, she dizzily drew herself up the staircase.

Spots danced a malicious courante in front of her eyes. She swayed at the top of the stairs, and the porcelain basin slipped from her hands with a crash. The master bedroom door flew open, and Sarah felt herself lifted up.

''What's that racket?''

"Sir Randolph, no! You can't get out of bed."

"What's wrong with you?"

"Why . . . nothing," Sarah lied, trying to still the violent pounding in her head. *"I just slipped, that's all."*

He picked her up. Sarah felt her head lolling against the smooth expanse of his chest exposed through the open robe. *"Stop it,"* she said, panicking. *"I've already told you—"*

"Don't be a fool," he said impatiently. *"That's the last thing on my mind right now. You're sick with the plague."*

"No—I never get sick."

"Well, you are now. Did you think you had some kind of magic invulnerability that the rest of us don't have?"

He gazed down at her for a moment, and Sarah was shocked at the look of concern in his eyes. Sir Randolph? Sir Randolph didn't care a jot for anybody. She stirred in his arms, attempting to escape, but he carried her into the guest bedroom next to his own and laid her on the bed. *"Martha!"* he shouted. *"Where's Martha?"*

The housekeeper flew into the bedroom, her broad face alarmed under its starched white cap. *"Sir?"*

"The governess is ill. Is there any of the physician's potion left? Get it, and bring some water too."

Martha looked suitably frightened, Sarah saw through feverish eyes. "Be it the plague, sir?"

"Yes."

"Oh, sir... I don't know. I got three children of me own."

"What do I pay you for? You'll do it now or... never mind," *he said impatiently.* "Go home to your children—I'll do it myself."

Jenny shivered, pulling the rough blanket up closer. Her nose wrinkled at its musty aroma. The stars were fading now that the morning was drawing near. She was sorry to see them go. Along with her thoughts, they had been her only companions for hours.

Jenny warily pulled herself up to the fly-specked window and looked out. When she'd hidden in this cellar, she'd been terrified they would find her. Was it safe to come out now? She thought of her family, forgetting their strictness and remembering only their warmth. She thought of Lukas and hugged the dirty blanket, longing for his protective bulk to appear. She even thought of Edward—marriage with him would be infinitely better than staying in a cellar, she told herself.

Her eyes caught a flash of blue on her right shoulder, and she plucked the remnant of material from her shoulder. She trembled suddenly. If her scarf hadn't ripped, Rocky would have had her. He'd made the mistake of grabbing for the scarf instead of her when she'd twisted from his grip. She'd run faster than she'd ever believed she could. Even then, she'd only just had time to duck into this cellar before he and his companion had come pounding around the corner.

Feeling somewhat more confident now in the light of breaking dawn, Jenny decided to risk leaving. She crouched low as she scrambled over the crumbling bricks and through the door. Then her heart froze in her chest as she stumbled into a huge form that swept her off her feet.

"Lukas!"

He looked down at Jenny, and a wave of longing swept over her. Her body leaned into his, and he kissed her quickly, then held her away from him as if he was afraid he wouldn't be able to stop. A wave of regret swept over her when he pulled away from the kiss.

"Did they hurt you?" he asked furiously after Jenny managed to tell him what had happened.

"I'm all right."

Her thoughts were jumbled as Lukas, his arm around her shoulder, ushered her out to the street. She'd been expecting a police car, and her eyebrows rose at the sight of the beat-up Trans Am. Lukas must be off duty, she decided. It was his own car, of course. She slid into the front seat with undisguised relief.

"Your family has been up all night," Lukas told her. "They're frantic with worry."

Jenny looked regretfully at Lukas. What she really wanted to tell him was that she loved him. But how could she tell him that? Lukas had rescued her because she had rescued him, she realized. Now they were even. It was a matter of honor to Lukas, not one of love.

"I told you that you didn't realize how dangerous Rocky and his friends are," Lukas said softly. "They smuggle drugs internationally, and there's nothing they'd like better than to latch on to a shipping line with a respected name."

His eyes flared with anger, and Jenny wondered why he was so concerned. But any cop would be upset at the thought of drug smuggling, she reminded herself.

He stared suddenly at her dejected form. "I've got to get to the station first. We can phone your family from there."

Jenny quailed. It was true—he couldn't wait to be rid of her. Lukas's thoughts were already plunging ahead, she saw. He was flexing and unflexing his big hands with what looked like impatience.

Jenny didn't reply. When they got to the police station, Lukas barely spared her a second glance.

"I've got to let everyone know what's happened. Wait here." Jenny sat down in the waiting area he indicated and found herself overwhelmed by self-pity. She stared at the wall until her face suddenly tightened. She sprang up and stalked to the pay phones.

"Jenny! You're all right?" her father exclaimed when he heard her voice.

Jenny reassured her father and explained what had happened. "I'm sure the police will be talking to you later," she said.

"Edward is here too. We'll be right down to get you."

"What are you doing?" Lukas's voice came from right behind her.

Jenny jumped. "I'll see you then," she said into the receiver, and hung up. "I've just phoned my family."

"I can take you home now."

"My . . . father is coming to get me." Jenny didn't mention Edward, though she knew he was with her father too.

"It would be quicker if I drove you."

"No . . . he wants me to wait."

Lukas frowned. "What's with your family? Don't they trust anybody?"

"My family is very conservative," she said lamely.

"I'll say," Lukas snapped. "Has anyone told them there's no longer an emperor in China?"

Jenny colored at the taunt. She tossed her head angrily. "They're not *that* conservative—and they've always been very good to me."

"So good you'd rather be with them . . . is that it?" Lukas looked at her challengingly.

Jenny felt confused. All her life she had been taught to respect her family's wishes. But this man made her feel as though he and he alone could fill the aching void he had opened in her heart. Until Lukas had come along, she hadn't realized such a gap existed in her comfortable life. Would just writing about romance be enough after this?

"I am to be married," she said dully. "It was all arranged a long time ago."

"Well, why don't you unarrange it?" Lukas slammed the wall with a closed fist, and Jenny jumped. "It doesn't have to be that way anymore!"

But did it? Jenny wondered. Even if her obligation to marry Edward somehow disappeared, she knew her great-grandmother would never approve of her marrying a policeman. Jenny suddenly wondered why she was even assuming Lukas was interested in marriage.

Why, she realized with an unpleasant twinge, he had never said he was. Her consternation grew. Lukas had abandoned her in the waiting area without a second glance, she remembered. Was that how he treated women?

"Oh, why did you have to be a cop?" she exploded suddenly.

Lukas gave her a puzzled look. "Look, I know how

your great-grandmother feels about policemen, but it's not—''

''They'll be here soon,'' Jenny said with despair choking her voice. ''I—I . . . thank you and . . . good-bye.''

''Thanks, but no thanks.'' His black eyebrows drew into a thunderous line. ''Now I get it—you can't stand the thought of your precious family catching you at something human, can you? Were you just out for a quick fling before you settled down with a proper husband? Was that what I was to you?''

Lukas started toward her, and Jenny backed away. He grabbed her viciously and kissed her, pressing his lips over her mouth as if he wanted to leave their imprint there forever. Jenny couldn't help it. She struggled against her newfound passion, but it won an easy victory. She began to return the kiss.

But Lukas withdrew his lips as suddenly as he had taken hers. He gripped her wrists for a moment and then thrust her away. ''Remember that in your new home,'' he said, and stalked away.

Jenny slumped. Her body ached with its need for him, but it was too late. Her father—and Edward—would soon be at the station.

She realized suddenly how things must appear to Lukas—that she was only leading him on. No wonder he hated her, Jenny thought with self-disgust. She hadn't had a chance to tell him about her promise to the Old One. It was too late, she thought again. Lukas despised her now.

Sarah felt devastated once he had actually gone. Oh, why had she flown into such a temper? The picnic with the children had been wonderful, and Sir Randolph had actually laughed when young Richard had leaned too far forward and tumbled into the duck pond.

Whatever had possessed her to mention his late wife? His face had instantly darkened, its displeasure visible even in the deep shade under the giant elms. Without saying a word, he had left them.

Heedless of the quarreling children, she stared now at the horse and rider fleeing over the stony fields. Was Sir Randolph going to that woman? For the first time, she looked down at her serviceable dress with distaste. Lady Penelope was a lady, and Sarah was not. Of course he'd find her a suitable match, Sarah thought unhappily. She was nothing—was something he had clutched at in the manner that a baby grabbed for a rattle—something easily cast aside when a more entrancing plaything was spotted. She had nothing to hold him. Her love meant nothing to him.

Chapter Seven

"It'll be the biggest hit since Bryan Adams went platinum," Ben said enthusiastically. He strode excitedly about Jenny's bedroom, his long fingers threading restlessly through his hair.

"It's wonderful news, Ben." Jenny managed a smile, not wanting to dampen her brother's happiness. She knew how long and hard he had worked for this day. A record contract with a big company like Moby Productions was cause for celebration. Even the Old One had grudgingly admitted that Ben had done well.

"You should have been there, Jenny. The agent warned us that nothing might come of it, that they were only interested in hearing how we played . . . but once the demo tape was done and the big bosses got a listen, we were in—just like that,'' he said wonderingly.

"It wasn't just good luck." Jenny felt much older and wiser than her brother. "You've been working hard at your music for years."

Ben stopped his excited pacing and considered her words. "A lot of people do that," he said suddenly. "But not everybody gets a break at the right time." He looked earnestly at his sister. "When something does come along, you have to go for it."

Touché, Jenny thought weakly. Ben was right. All the hard work in the world could be in vain if you dropped the ball at the wrong moment. Or if you refused to pick it up. She smiled, somewhat sourly, remembering her conversation with Lynn. It seemed that she also had cause to celebrate. Her agent had said the senior editor was entranced by *Noblesse Oblige.* Especially, she blushingly recalled, its love scenes.

"You've never written like that before," Lynn said admiringly when she phoned to congratulate her. "I know I suggested you warm it up, but oh, Jenny . . . I had to fan myself every time they were in a room together."

"I'm glad you like it, Lynn," Jenny said dryly.

"Liked it? I loved it! For sure this is going to be the biggest print run ever." A crafty note crept into her voice. "Don't take this wrong, but I can hardly wait to see what you're going to write like *after* you're married.'' Jenny winced, but Lynn's shrill voice suddenly softened. ''Sorry about that other bit.''

''That's okay, Lynn. It was just a thought.''

''It wasn't a bad idea, Jenny. But putting bloomers into a period romance just didn't work. You don't have to make your heroine so feisty that she single-handedly invents comfortable clothing for women centuries before anyone else. That's a bit too much for people to believe. But the love scenes . . .'' And Lynn had been off again.

Jenny wondered now if she'd be able to write at all after her marriage to Edward. Every touch, every lingering kiss that she had shared with Lukas had gone into her latest book. Could those memories survive a life shared with someone else? She doubted Edward's ungenerous ego would make room for the notion that his wife might have a mind of her own.

In three short days, they would be married. Jenny wrenched her mind away from the disturbing thought. ''It's wonderful,'' she told her brother again. ''I'm really happy for you.''

Ben's face suddenly sobered. ''Look, I should be the one thanking you. What you went through—''

''It's all right.'' Jenny hushed him. She didn't want to think of Lukas—to remember his powerful arms or relive the experience of leaning into his smooth chest. She had exorcised her love, banished it to the pages of her book so that others could look forward to something she would never have. Her future, like a barren plot of land, stretched out dismally in front of her. Jenny saw clearly now what it would be: marriage with a man she didn't love, quiet obedience, and a back-row seat in Edward's life.

"I've got to get dressed now." She gave Ben a hug and he left the room, still walking on air as he happily considered his impending stardom.

The day would be a hot one, she saw. The east rays of the sun slanted across the bed and suddenly touched her body, reminding her of warm fingers. Jenny slipped out of her nightgown and stared dejectedly at her closet. Edward was coming to visit today, she remembered. The family would not be impressed if she wore jeans.

After she showered, Jenny powdered herself with a faintly orange-smelling talc. She took a pair of casual shorts from her drawer and then made herself put them back. Her hand drifted over the rows of hangers. It stopped, darting in to select a fiery orange sundress. Jenny pulled the garment over her head, reflecting that a quiet hour or two in the garden might raise her spirits. The color was certainly cheering, she thought as she studied the vibrant reflection in the mirror.

The sleeveless dress was stretch cotton. It was set off by zippered pockets and a cutwork pattern of petals that circled her neck, giving glimpses of the creamy skin beneath. Jenny stroked her lips with a brush, applying tangerine gloss. She slid her damp hair back into a broad orange silk band. Liking the monochrome effect, she stepped into a pair of strappy sandals. The leather uppers were a brown-orange that complemented the vibrant color of the dress. A touch of orange-colored blush to her cheekbones and a light coat of mascara to her eyelashes and Jenny felt that her misery was suitably disguised. *Time to greet the day,* she thought gloomily.

Downstairs, her mother was rushing to make her way through a list of last-minute details for the wedding. "Didn't anybody think to order ice?" she said, exasperated. "Really, this is supposed to be a professional caterer."

From behind her mother's shoulder, Jenny scrutinized the snowstorm of papers spread on the elegant writing desk. "The blue one," she suggested.

"Where?" Her mother looked confused, and then her hand fumbled the blue paper out from an overlooked stack. "Oh, good," she said, putting a slim hand up to straighten an elegant coiffure that needed no straightening. "Jenny, I'm so nervous I feel like I'm the one who's getting married. How in the world are you managing to stay so calm and collected?"

Her mother, not waiting for a reply, got up and hurried down the hall to the kitchen as though demons were after her. Jenny smiled sadly. What was there for her to be nervous about? Her life was over, so nothing really mattered much one way or the other.

She drifted out to the garden. She frowned when she saw that even this sanctuary had been disturbed by the frenzied preparations for the wedding. The bower where she liked to sit and read had been moved and placed in the center of the neatly manicured lawn. Boxes of red party lanterns were scattered haphazardly over the patio, and stacks of long tables, newly arrived from the caterer, were being set up by two men in white coveralls.

Jenny suddenly remembered the fish pond. She turned from the confused scene ahead of her and slipped around the side of the house. The pleasant little pond was a fish pond in name only. Once, when Jenny was thirteen, it had been home to Ben's clan of turtles. Jenny knelt at its edge, remembering the ridiculous carp in another fish pond. What a spectacular evening that had been, she thought. Until it ended in disaster, she amended.

''Did you need quiet time, too?''

Jenny shot up, startled, and she spied her great-grandmother sitting on a bench in the shade of an ornamental cherry tree. ''I thought you were helping Mother.''

''I'm just in the way now,'' the Old One said complacently. She lowered her voice to a conspiratorial whisper. ''Your mother is impossible to deal with.''

Jenny smiled. She too had been trying hard for the past two days to stay out of her panicking mother's way. The countless details of the wedding were beginning to exhaust even her mother's usually patient efficiency.

"What were you thinking about?"

"Life . . . death. Yin and yang." Her great-grandmother's eyes were dreamy, Jenny saw. "They were principles put in place by men, you know. Yang is light, heaven, and warmth—the south side of the mountain. Yin is dark, earthy, and cold—the north side of the mountain."

"I've always wondered why women are yin and men are yang."

Her great-grandmother regarded her humorously. "I just said the great principles were put in place by men."

Jenny laughed. "That would explain it," she admitted. "Great-grandmother?"

"Yes, child?"

"Why did they bind women's feet in the old days?"

The Old One sighed. "Men grew to like it, I suppose. And no wife with her feet bound was likely to run away. The men used to carry them piggyback like bundles when they had to go a long distance."

"They must have been very insecure," Jenny suggested. "No man nowadays would resort to such measures to keep a woman with him."

Her great-grandmother's eyes raised inquisitively. She smiled, seemingly at the surety of Jenny's statement, and gave her a speculative look. "Men have always used whatever means they have at their disposal to keep the things—or the women—they want. It's their *chi*—the vital energy that comes from within. Why do you ask, Jenny?"

"Just curious," Jenny said. *Because of the dream,* she thought. The recurrent dream was disturbing her sleep. Each time she dreamed she was standing beside Edward, who was seated at a table. He was talking on his mobile telephone and ignoring her completely. A bowl of sharks' fin soup was cooling in front of him. A sense of impending doom would come over her, and she would try to warn Edward, but discover she was unable to speak. Then she would realize she was rooted to the spot. The dream ended each time with Jenny staring down at her feet to discover that they were only three inches long. Horror-struck, she would wake up. The first time she had actually checked her feet to make sure they were unchanged.

"You'll be all right," the Old One said. "Don't be nervous about the marriage. It will be a big change for you, but a glorious one after you have children."

"I hope so," Jenny said fervently.

"It will make you happy," her great-grandmother insisted. "These days the three bonds of obedience are no longer harsh ones."

Jenny's ears pricked up. That certainly sounded ominous. "What are they?"

"The three bonds were what controlled women from the day of their birth to the day of their death in the old days. Women were expected to obey their fathers when they were young, their husbands when married, and their adult sons if they were widowed."

"You never do anything Father wants," Jenny protested and laughed.

The Old One smiled. "But I honor him," she said. "He has worked very hard to expand the family's business. Running the household is something else again." She sniffed. "Look at your mother's silly ideas about this wedding. A small wedding, she said— there's over three hundred guests. Don't worry, Jenny—you'll be a good wife."

"I'll do my best, Great-grandmother."

A maid, looking as if she was searching for someone, came around the corner. A look of relief spread across her face when she saw the Old One.

"Oldest One, you're needed. Your granddaughter-in-law humbly requests your assistance with the seating arrangements."

"Help me up," the Old One sighed. "Are you coming, Jenny?"

"No, Great-grandmother. I think I'd like to stay here for a while." Jenny had no intention of being drawn into the battle of who would sit where during the wedding banquet.

"Smart girl," the Old One said with a grumble.

Jenny ducked her head and smiled. Her great-grandmother had instantly divined her reason, she knew.

"Your mother will have put all of her relatives at the head table, and I'll have to correct that now."

Jenny remained diplomatically silent. She smiled with satisfaction as her great-grandmother tottered around the corner, helped by the maid. Now she had her favorite corner all to herself.

Jenny pounced on the bench vacated by the Old One and put a pillow under her head. She had not risen until ten o'clock, but she was still tired. Unable to sleep properly since the dream came, she had been taking more and more catnaps during the quickly passing days. She shut her eyes, feeling the hot pinpricks of the sun squeezing through the leaves. She remembered how his kisses had set fire to her upturned face. . . .

. . . A pair of rubbery leeches had attached themselves to her mouth and were sucking the life out of her. . . . Jenny's eyes flew open, but the nightmare didn't end. It got worse—Edward was kissing her. She pushed him away with one spasmodic shove. Blinking at the sun overhead, she realized that she had slept the morning away.

"Sleeping Beauty didn't push Prince Charming away," Edward said. He looked as though he were going to kiss her again, and Jenny sat up hastily.

"You scared me," she said accusingly. She ran a hand through her hair and stood up to leave. Edward moved to stand in front of her. Jenny's startled eyes noticed there was anger in his.

"Aren't we ever going to spend some time together before the wedding? There's no reason to wait anymore. We could be celebrating now."

His hands caught at her shoulders, and Jenny felt herself drawn toward him. Resisting, she broke away. "I . . . I have to use the washroom," she said, uttering the first excuse that came into her head.

But Edward grabbed her again, and this time her struggles were in vain. Her feet funneled tracks in the grass as her tense body was pulled toward him. "You're my wife," he said flatly, "and you'll do whatever I want."

"I believe the lady said she wanted to use the facilities," a male voice said.

Jenny was abruptly released. Lukas, wearing a suit that was expensively subtle—its narrow lapels dipped in a manner that she recognized as Savile Row tailoring—strode forward. Edward looked curiously fawning, Jenny thought. Was he afraid Lukas would hit him? It was not the look of a man with a right to his mate.

"What are you doing here?"

Lukas smiled at Jenny's tremulous question. His eyes were warm. "I've come to tell you the good news. Rocky and his friends are in jail."

"That's wonderful," Jenny said with a relieved smile. "We saw the news of the raid in the newspaper, but it didn't mention names. Will . . . will I have to testify?"

She looked worriedly at Edward. Inwardly, her heart leaped.

"Probably not," Lukas said. "But I might have to haul you in for questioning." Amazingly, he winked. Jenny stared at him, nonplussed. Her eyes rose to examine his suit. Where would a cop come up with the money for a thousand-dollar suit? A nagging fear rose in her mind. Was Lukas a crooked cop?

"Why are you dressed like that?" she asked hesitantly.

"Do you like it?" Lukas said. His eyes were amused. "I've been working for my father this weekend, and he insisted I get rid of the jeans—didn't you say you needed to use the bathroom?"

"Ah, yes." Jenny glanced quickly at Edward and began walking to the house. She stared back curiously as she rounded the corner. The two men were talking. It looked like a deep discussion, and she wished she could hear them. Edward was nodding, seemingly agreeing with everything Lukas said.

In her bathroom, Jenny scrubbed at her lips and brushed her teeth too, erasing all memory of Edward's kiss. Her heart sang. She brushed her hair back briskly, binding its shining fullness with an ebony hair clasp. The hair band, she decided, made her look like too much of a schoolgirl.

As she methodically reapplied her makeup, Jenny's thoughts were in a whirl. What was Lukas really doing here? she wondered. He could have easily spoken to her father by phone. And just what did his father do that he needed to wear a suit like that to work for him? He couldn't be a policeman too . . . not if he could afford to buy his son a suit like that.

Jenny wondered if she should change her dress, and decided against it. Edward might get the wrong idea and think she was trying to impress him. Her face fell. Oh, why was she having so much trouble remembering? It was Edward she was going to marry, not Lukas.

Lukas, she remembered unhappily, thought she was a wimp. He had as much as accused her of that. She knew the kind he meant—the sort of woman who insisted on marrying a man with social position so she could live in luxurious security. *Why, I'd be happy in a bare cave if I could have Lukas,* Jenny thought sadly. She had a ludicrous vision of herself writing romance novels in a cave. *Why not?* she thought crazily. *I could support us both.*

When she returned downstairs she spotted Lukas in

deep conversation with her great-grandmother. She looked searchingly about, but could see no sign of Edward.

''Where's Edward gone?'' she asked, puzzled.

''A business tip he had to act on right away came up,'' Lukas said smoothly. Her great-grandmother's hand rose to cover her mouth. Lukas got up from his chair and bowed to the Old One. He stared admiringly at Jenny. ''You aren't too disappointed, I hope.''

His amber eyes glinted knowingly at her improved appearance, and Jenny flushed. ''He might have stayed to tell me himself,'' she shot back, disliking his ability to read her so well.

''Is his absence always such a hardship to you then?'' Lukas asked daringly.

Jenny, her mouth opening with astonishment at his nerve, turned to her great-grandmother. But strangely, the Old One seemed untouched by any sense that what he had just said was improper. Instead, she said something else. Something amazing.

''Why don't you both go for a walk? Jenny's father won't be home for another hour.''

Jenny was absolutely rigid with disbelief. It was as if the sun and the moon had traded places. First her family wouldn't allow her out on her own, and now her great-grandmother was practically throwing her into the arms of a man who wasn't her fiancé! As if in a dream, she felt Lukas take her arm and guide her outside.

He opened the door of a silver Ferrari, and Jenny's eyes widened. Wordlessly, she got inside. "Do you like it?" Lukas asked. "I just bought it."

Just bought it? Jenny's eyes traveled over the wood-grained dashboard and the leather seats. It wasn't just any Ferrari, she realized uneasily. It was a limited edition, something Ben would give his eyeteeth to own.

"It's very nice," she said icily. Inside, Jenny felt on the brink of despair. Had Lukas, after engineering what the newspapers were calling the biggest smuggling bust of the decade, gone crooked? Was this where his supposed belief that she was infatuated with money had led him?

Jenny ducked her head, refusing to answer the deeper question in his eyes.

"Let's go to Stanley Park, shall we?" he said after a moment. His voice held a teasing note, and Jenny remembered that he had once said he wanted to take her to a romantic spot in the park. Jenny couldn't help it. Every fiber of her being was aware of his presence in the next seat.

Sitting next to him was a form of torture, Jenny thought with dismay. Her eyes slid to his legs. *What beautiful pants,* she thought. *No,* a back corner of her mind insisted—*you mean what gorgeous legs!* Jenny forced her eyes up with an effort and looked out the window. Lukas was taking the long way through the city, she noticed. Was he afraid to talk to her? She darted a quick look at him. *No, not him,* she thought. *He looks as confident as a stockbroker.*

Staring out at the beautiful day—what other city boasted the Pacific Ocean, islands, mountains, and green expanses all in the same view?—Jenny found herself relaxing a bit. She caught herself grinning at the matched pair of lions that sat on pedestals on either side of the aging Lions Gate Bridge. A similar stone pair graced the front gates of Sir Randolph's country estate.

"Is that all you want?" Sarah asked sarcastically.

His amber eyes blazed suddenly, and Sarah dropped her head, unable to meet the intensity of Sir Randolph's gaze. "You take care of my children, run the household . . . why is it you've never thought of my needs?"

He was impossible, Sarah thought. "You're not a child!" she protested. "Far from it!" She rose from the chair and paced restlessly to the window. Outside, the rugged hills were ablaze with heather. A shepherd and his baaing flock tripped across the ancient stone bridge, heading for the cottage on the east side of the moor. Sarah knew she'd miss this place. And the children too.

She darted a quick look at his insolent face. How

she hated him! But there was no help for it. Sir Randolph had trapped her, and she was boxed in a corner from which there was no escape. Either Sarah had connubial relations with him or her stay at Greystones was at an end.

"It's unbearable!" Sir Randolph shouted. "You are the most impossible woman. Why in the world won't you marry me?"

Sarah's heart felt as though it had been split in two. "Marry you?" She faltered. "But I thought . . ."

Waiting for a bicycle built for two—they were a popular rental item with tourists—to pump across the crosswalk before pulling the car forward into the park, Lukas began humming. Jenny felt irritated by his continuing good humor. She wished she had something to be happy about. How could he turn to crime when she already loved him for himself? Jenny blushed, unable to forget that it was currently not love at a safe distance. She stared at the crowds, wondering how many people would be witnessing the sight of her telling him off.

Lukas continued down the narrow highway that meandered through the wooded hills of the park. The cool breeze sighed through the grove of trees, bringing the pungent scent of cedar into the car. Lukas steered the car off the road and into an obscure parking lot Jenny had never been in before. Despite the crowds elsewhere, the lot was empty of other vehicles. They were at the north end of the park—the wild side that most found the least attractive. A narrow path plunged from the edge of the asphalt into the fir and pine trees below.

"Down here," Lukas said. He gestured for her to follow him. They moved single-file down the narrow path. Jenny's feet were cushioned by the layers of pine needles built up over years. Her feet crunched down, releasing a fragrant burst at every step. Blocked from seeing what was up ahead by the immense size of his back, Jenny wondered where Lukas was taking her. The trail slanted down sharply, and she was just able to manage it in her high-heeled shoes.

To Jenny's relief, the path soon leveled out. They walked steadily for some minutes until the pine needles under their feet gave way, first to spongy moss and then to smooth rock. When they stopped, Jenny was delighted to see that they were standing on a ledge that ran raggedly out into the water. Its farthest point disappeared into the ocean beyond.

"It's lovely." *A bit eerie, though,* she thought to herself. She gazed upward at the silently outstretched arms of the ruddy, thick-barked trees. They were mature cedars, hung with spaghnum moss as gray and as fragile as old bird nests.

"You see that rock?" Lukas pointed to a black rock jutting from the water. Polished smooth by the pounding waves, the rock stood lonely vigil in the swooping waters of the inlet. ''That's Pauline Johnson's rock.''

''What?'' Jenny said. ''You mean the Indian poetess?'' She peered at the solitary rock with renewed interest, remembering the poems she had read in school. A seagull, keening, swept past the lonely rock and disappeared into the water.

They clambered closer to the point, and Lukas raised his voice against the crashing of the waves.

''Legend has it that she loved a man . . . a white trader who met her when the coastal Indians were still living here in cedar lodges.''

''I've never heard this story,'' Jenny shouted, cupping her ears. ''What happened?''

''One day he didn't return. She waited for him on this ledge, searching the waters for him every day. He never came back, and she pined away and died. She's buried in this park. But the Indians say her spirit went into that rock . . . that she's still waiting for him to return.''

Jenny stared at the rock. It was about the size of a human being, she realized. Was that how the legend had started? She shivered and made her way back to the path. ''That's not a very happy story,'' she told Lukas when he caught up to her.

''Sometimes stories have sad endings,'' Lukas said. He moved closer. ''But they don't have to be sad.'' His lips met Jenny's, and she almost swooned at their pressure and the remembered impact. Lukas clasped her hands and brought them up to his chest. He gently squeezed them and released her lips.

"Jenny . . . if you weren't going to marry Edward Li, would you marry me?"

"I . . . what kind of a question is that?" Jenny tried to deny the aching throb of her heart. She looked away, but saw only the lonely rock in the water. She blinked. Had she seen it move?

"Yes or no," Lukas said urgently. "If you were free, would you marry me?"

Jenny couldn't stop herself. "Yes," she whispered. Then she pulled away from the man she was aching to touch. Careless of her high heels, she ran up the path. A piece of spaghnum moss touched her on the shoulder, and she flinched from its ghostly touch. The breeze seemed to have followed her from the ocean. It churned in the air like an endless whisper. Stumbling, she clapped her hands over her ears and broke through the trees to the parking lot. She stood panting by the car, her heart beating wildly, trying to pull herself together before Lukas appeared.

She had promised . . . she had promised. Where was her honor? Her family must never know what she had told Lukas.

When he caught up with her, Lukas reached for Jenny. "I've got to get back," she said quickly, before he could touch her. "I've got a pounding headache."

''Shall we stop and get you something?''

''No . . . I just want to get home.'' Her eyes fell again on his suit, and she turned away. Lukas captured her hand, but she pulled angrily away. He was involved in something illegal. How could she have slipped like that and admitted what she felt for him?

Jenny got into the car and put a hand to her head. A headache was starting in earnest, she realized. She thought of the lonely point of rock and wondered if she'd been cursed. It was silly, she knew, but that place had bothered her—put her on edge. What was that woman from another time, another culture, trying to tell her?

''You're really suffering, aren't you?'' Lukas gave her a sympathetic look.

''Yes,'' she said quietly. Why had Lukas asked her if she would marry him? To gauge the extent of his power over her? Didn't he realize how difficult things were for her already? By the time the car had pulled into the concrete driveway of her family's deceptively modern-looking home, Jenny was completely miserable.

She pulled away from Lukas when they reached the top of the steps and blindly opened the door. Without a word she ran for the stairs, cursing his masculine arrogance in forcing her to admit her love for him. It was nothing she would ever be allowed to express—

except on paper, she reminded herself bitterly—and he knew it. How could he torture her like that?

Sobbing, she flew up the steps, past her surprised great-grandmother, who was being helped across the foyer by a maid.

"Brides"—she heard the Old One say to Lukas—"they're nothing but nerves with a bit of skin on top."

Chapter Eight

*T*he church bells pealed out merrily over the commons as they departed the church. Sarah caught her breath at the sight of the cheering villagers turned out to greet them.

They had decorated the carriage with bouquets of wildflowers. Sprigs of heather stuck out from every wheel, and even the matched pair of bays wore crowns of wreathed flowers. Sarah smiled at them all, exposing even, white teeth that did not go unnoticed.

"S'death," she heard one old cottager mumble sadly, "it's the way of the world, I always said. Thems that has them, doesn't needs them."

Sarah laughed gaily, calling out a promise to visit his cottage and bring him some of the soft bread from *the manor kitchens. She looked happily about her. She wanted to share her good fortune, and there were so many things she could do now! She studied the people with pleased interest. Some of the children were alert-looking, despite their rags. Why not a school?*

She turned to her smiling husband and looked at him with pleading eyes. "What now?" he said, pretending gruffness.

"Have you ever thought of how useful these people would be if they were trained to do more than work the estate? The land is not enough to feed them. Most are forced to travel from village to village at harvest-time to keep their families from starving. If they got some schooling, don't you think they'd be a help to you?"

Sir Randolph hesitated. "I don't want them to get ideas above their station. What kind of schooling did you have in mind?"

"The women could learn to weave. The men . . . Oh, I don't know," she said impatiently. "There's brick-making and glassblowing and all kinds of trades in the village I came from."

"Let's talk about it later."

"But you'll consider it?" she asked eagerly. "The vicar has already agreed to help." She rose on tiptoes and hugged him around the waist. His hands slipped to her own tightly corseted waist and drew her to him.

"I promise—let's not keep the villagers waiting any

longer. They've worked for three days on the wedding feast.''

Jenny reluctantly put the galleys down. The book was finished, right down to the corrections, but the thought gave her no pleasure. Instead, she felt hollow inside. She went to the bedroom window and looked out. A light breeze was merrily chasing a few wayward clouds from the impossibly blue sky. The forecast of rain had proved wrong, and the canopies hadn't been needed after all. It was a day that any bride should be grateful to have for her wedding.

The banquet tables were in place, and the catering staff had finished placing a set of gold cutlery and a linen napkin in front of each chair. A carpenter was still busy putting the last touches on a set of steps leading up to the transformed bower. Her mother was fluttering about him like a bird with a broken wing, begging him to hurry.

Sighing, Jenny removed the red dress of happiness from the closet. The other dresses had been pulled aside, giving it an honored spot by itself in the center of the closet. Jenny studied its straight and uncompromising lines and sighed again. The activity in the hall below her bedroom had risen to a furious pitch. The guests were arriving. She could delay no longer. It was time to put it on.

Jenny undid the bobbles and slipped the dress over

her head. She did the side of the dress up slowly and smoothed the tight dress into place. She stared at the unknown woman in the mirror. The red satin shone, and the narrow, tubular shape of the traditional wedding dress emphasized her small-boned figure. Jenny turned, still looking at herself in the full-length mirror. She was numbly aware that she had never looked more desirable in her life.

Her mother soon bustled into the room, ending her last moment of solitude. Trailed by two maids, she looked totally efficient, totally in control, and—to Jenny's mind—totally exhausted. It had all been a herculean effort for her, Jenny thought. Her mother would probably sleep for twelve hours after it was all over.

"A house could be built in the time it took that man to put three steps together," she complained. "Oh, good . . . you've got it on. Let's get your hair done."

Jenny sat carefully at the dressing room table, and her mother set to work, her fingers flying with pins over Jenny's glossy head. She stood back to stare at the style when she was finished, judging it as though it were a painting. Upswept and pinned into place, the effect was sophisticated, Jenny thought, but her mother was not finished. She motioned to the maids. Bowing, one held out a black lacquered box. The other opened the lid. Jenny's breath caught in her throat as her mother lifted out a glittering headdress. Its red silk veil was embroidered with gold tinsel. Miniature strands of pearls and tiny golden balls dangled from the top. Her mother fitted it carefully over Jenny's shining hair and anchored the headdress with pins. Jenny's eyes widened as she caught sight of herself in the mirror.

"Where in the world did it come from, Mother?" Jenny moved her head from side to side and heard the tiny tinkling of bells.

"The Old One," her pleased mother replied. "She wore it, and her mother before her wore it, and hers before her. It's very old . . . but beautiful, don't you think?"

Jenny did. She raised a wondering hand to her forehead and pushed the veil aside. She heard the click of canes and twisted her head in the direction of the sound. She smiled at the Old One, who looked as pleased as if she were wearing the wonderful headdress herself.

"Do you like it?" the Old One asked. She surveyed her great-granddaughter with satisfaction. "One of my ancestors was a lady-in-waiting at the Imperial Court. She would have looked much as you do, I imagine."

"It's really beautiful, Great-grandmother. Thank you for thinking of me. I . . . I feel like a queen."

And Jenny did feel like a queen—from her reading and research into the historical backgrounds she used for her books, she knew full well that the queens of all nations were never allowed to marry whom they

wanted. She stared at the regal headdress, wondering
about the women who had worn it before her. Had any
of them married the men they loved? Her head
dropped.

She saw that the Old One was staring approvingly
at her.

"It's proper for a bride to be modest," her great-
grandmother said. "And now I'd like a moment with
my great-granddaughter alone."

"Nonsense," Jenny's mother said stiffly. "The
child's barely dressed."

"Oh . . . by the way, the carpenter wanted to know
where the carpet was so he can put it on the stairs,"
the Old One said. "I told him not to bother. There's
been too much fuss over this wedding already."

"You what!" Jenny's mother flew from the room,
the maids following in her frenetic wake.

Jenny giggled. The bells tinkled like accompanying
laughter.

"Never mind your mother," the Old One said
tartly. "Are you ready, Jenny?"

Jenny knew she wasn't talking about her appearance. "I don't think change is the kind of thing you
can ever be ready for," she told her seriously.

"Now you're becoming a woman," the Old One said
with satisfaction. "I remember my own wedding . . .
my tears at being married to a man who was thirty

years my senior. I had a terrible time of it—that's not going to happen to you.''

"I hope not, Great-grandmother.''

"Marriage to a highly respected man is a very different prospect from my sale to the lout who caused my feet to be bound.'' She looked passionately at Jenny. "Such is not to be the fate of my great-granddaughter.''

What was she getting at? Jenny hated it when she was mysterious. "Did you love my grandfather?'' she asked suddenly.

"Love like a bolt from the heavens comes to few . . . your grandfather rescued me from an unhappy fate, and I grew to love him after I realized that he truly loved me. I was happy to bear his children and glad to serve at his side until the day he died. He was rich with honor, beloved by his children and grandchildren and all the members of his ministry when he died.''

A maid came in and spoke briefly with the Old One.

"All your mother's fussing was for nothing,'' the Old One told Jenny. "The pastries turned out fine and all of the guests have arrived.''

Jenny's heart gave a mighty thump. *So soon?* she thought.

Her mother flew back into the room. "Oh, Jenny . . .'' She bent and hugged her carefully to avoid creasing her dress. "It's time.''

Jenny drew the two pieces of the veil together. She

rose gingerly and followed as the women made a grand procession from the room. Taking the tiny steps dictated by custom—and by the tight restrictions of the dress—she kept her eyes on the floor. In fact, she found it was something she had to do in order to keep moving forward—the gauzy veil was thicker than she had supposed. Jenny could scarcely see more than shadowy figures unless she stared at the ground. The headdress was part of a tradition that had once shielded the bride from the sight of the bridegroom until he parted the veil, surveying her for the first time when they were alone together in the marriage chamber. Jenny wondered how those women had borne it. Things hadn't changed all that much, she thought unhappily. She still had to wed Edward.

She tried desperately to think of her future children, but had difficulty imagining their faces. Instead, an image of a man with masterful eyebrows and glinting amber eyes rose up to haunt her.

Jenny heard the rising murmur of voices as the guests stood back, making room for the grand procession of the bride. She was led into the bright sunshine to the place of honor—the bower had been strung with red roses, and its customary bench had been replaced by a red-carpeted platform on which rested a small altar. She bowed stiffly. Then she knelt, averting her eyes from the bridegroom at her side, and waited for the ceremony to begin.

Acrid incense filled the air, along with chanting. Jenny made her responses automatically, uncomfortably aware of the form kneeling next to her. She felt numb with horror. Her ears rang. Edward seemed bigger, more threatening, and she wondered again how she would be able to bear her wedding night. That thousands of unhappy brides had borne it in the old days was little consolation to her now. Jenny's head remained modestly down, but inside her thoughts were caught up in a whirl of apprehension.

She dared to part her veil slightly and saw the Old One staring at her intently. *Now what?* she wondered desperately. *Haven't I done everything correctly?* A tear squeezed from her eye, and she let the veil drop.

It was done. The bridegroom withdrew, and Jenny rose gracefully. She was led back through a sea of unfamiliar faces that parted to allow her through. Shouts of best wishes rang out amidst the snapping of firecrackers set off to frighten away any jealous demons that might be lurking about.

As Jenny passed through the throng of guests, she raised her arms. Bracelets of eighteen-carat gold were thrust onto her outstretched arms. Other well-wishers placed necklaces of beaten gold over her head. Jenny's front and arms were soon a solid mass of shining gold. She politely turned around so the guests could inspect the full effect of the traditional gift. The jewelry blazed in the bright sunshine. Cameras snapped. Video recorders whirred. The guests roared their approval, and Jenny bowed. She righted herself with some difficulty because of the weight of the jewelry. But the weight was nothing compared with the stone on her heart.

Her mother approached, trailing maids. They surrounded her, giggling, and fingered the necklaces and bracelets with soft exclamations of delight. Once back in her bedroom, they carefully removed the jewelry and set it aside. It would later be put on display with the rest of the wedding gifts.

Jenny was helped out of the dress of happiness, and the cream-colored wedding dress was brought to her. Another round of frenzied dressing ensued. Her mother carefully removed the wonderful headdress. One maid offered her a cup of green tea, and Jenny sipped it as the others and her mother fussed with the six-foot train of her dress. A lace headdress was placed on her head, and her mother kissed her once for luck before pulling the translucent veil down over her daughter's face.

Then it was back out to the garden and back through the audience of chattering guests, who clapped heartily when they caught sight of the bride. Jenny was grateful for the concealing folds of the headdress. She blinked back tears as the minister droned on. It was too late to run, she realized with horror. What had she done? She was not only married to a man she didn't love, but now she was compounding the mistake by marrying him for a second time. She felt an iron despair descend to grip her heart. Her tears fell unnoticed under the veil.

"Do you, Lukas Hanh, take Jenny Lane to be your lawfully wedded wife, in sickness and in health and until death do you part?"

"I do," said the man beside her. Jenny's heart gave a convulsive leap. Her knees buckled, and a long arm shot out to support her. No longer caring what tradition she was breaking, she raised her veil with a trembling hand.

Lukas—his amber eyes filled with concern and mischief—smiled down at her. The minister grinned and said something.

"What?"

"Do you, Jenny Lane, take Lukas Hanh to be your lawfully wedded husband, in sickness and in health and until death do you part?"

"I got them to take out the 'obey' part," Lukas whispered. "I didn't think you'd like that much." He poked her. "Just answer the man." He squeezed her hand encouragingly.

"I—I do." Jenny thought she must be dreaming. Maybe she was still asleep and only imagining that she was marrying Lukas. Her astonished eyes sought her great-grandmother. There she was—sitting in the front row and looking remarkably pleased with herself. She returned Jenny's bewildered look with a smiling nod. Her brother grinned at her happily. Her parents beamed.

"I now pronounce you man and wife," the minister said heartily. "You may kiss the bride," he told Lukas. The prompting was unnecessary, for Lukas had already lifted her veil, and Jenny felt the grasp of his strong arms. He kissed her, his lips pressing against her surprised mouth. Jenny responded, clinging to him not with love, but with stupefaction.

Fireworks suddenly exploded in the garden and inside Jenny's heart. They kissed and kissed, and finally Lukas had to let her go so they could both pant for a moment. Lukas took her firmly, possessively, by the waist and led her down the steps of the platform.

Surrounded by smiling guests who offered their congratulations, Jenny managed a bewildered grin.

"Jenny, I'd like you to meet my parents," Lukas said, dragging her aside. "My father, Philip Hanh, and my mother, Janet Hanh—this is Jenny."

Jenny bowed automatically, her eyes rising to the graying man. He was as large as Lukas, she saw. Her eyes flashed to his mother, a petite woman impeccably turned out in a rose-silk suit. She liked her kind face instantly.

"And these are my sisters, Nancy and Selena." Two girls, petite and dainty like their mother, came shyly forward, and Jenny smiled suddenly. They were fourteen and sixteen years old, she learned. *What darlings,* she thought.

Jenny noticed her great-grandmother standing nearby. The Old One seemed to be staring with anxious relief at the petite female members of the Hanh family.

"My great-grandmother," she said, and made the formal introduction to Lukas's family. After everyone was introduced, the new family members stood and chatted. Lukas took her by the arm and urged her away to the head table.

"I thought you'd never look at me," he told her good-humoredly. "I always had the impression you were more interested in marriage than that." He pulled a chair out for her, and Jenny sat down with a thump.

"But how—"

"I talked with the Old One . . . but first I spoke with Edward." His eyes darkened momentarily and then returned to happy animation. They moved possessively over her, and Jenny felt a thrill shoot through her. "Your great-grandmother, believe it or not, was the easiest to convince. I told her she was making a big mistake marrying you off to a man like Edward. I told her that you'd never be happy with him." Lukas grasped her arm. "Would you?"

Jenny was confused. Her great-grandmother had agreed to break her betrothal? She looked up, alerted by the familiar click of canes. Lukas got up promptly and pulled out a second chair for the Old One. A beaming waiter offered his tray of white wine, and Jenny impatiently waved him away. *Maybe the Old One can give me some answers I can understand,* she thought.

"I've just been telling Jenny about our little talk. I'm not sure she believes me, honored great-grandmother."

"Humph," the Old One said. "Is it any surprise? Next time don't go along with what my daughter-in-law says and you'll be all right."

"Great-grandmother," Jenny said desperately, "what is going on?"

Jenny—I suppose you're the last person I should be telling this to—there are times when traditions have to be broken."

"You've never told me *that* before." Jenny looked at her accusingly.

"That's because the young should never think of such a thing," her great-grandmother said shortly. "With no experience they're hardly in a position to judge, are they?"

Jenny didn't know what to say. She smiled politely instead.

"Edward had had enough. What with you disappearing and then that awful risk you took at the docks . . . he decided life with you would be a more unsettling prospect than he had bargained for—especially after Lukas had a talk with him.''

The Old One arched her narrow eyebrows and looked at Lukas.

''I told him I'd break both his legs and hound his company into the ground if he held you to the betrothal,'' Lukas said pleasantly.

Irrationally, Jenny felt a moment's pique at the news of Edward's desertion. ''Why didn't he tell me the news himself?'' she demanded.

''As he was no longer your betrothed, it was no longer proper that he should speak to you,'' the Old One said smoothly. Her eyes danced, and she gave Jenny a penetrating look. ''Are you not pleased with second-best?'' She smiled knowingly.

But Jenny felt angry. It was the same way her family had served her with Edward. *Oh, but with a difference,* her heart sang out. But Jenny refused to listen. ''Don't I get a say?'' she asked. ''Nobody consulted me.''

Still smiling, her great-grandmother got up. ''See what you can do with this poor, mixed-up child,'' she told Lukas. She paused dramatically. ''After twenty-two years, I think it's high time for somebody else to help out.''

Lukas stood to help the Old One maneuver around the clutter of chairs. Then he looked down at Jenny's brooding face. She was staring at the wedding guests, realizing why so many of them looked unfamiliar. They would be Lukas's family members and friends, of course. They looked a prosperous bunch, she thought, an uneasy memory tickling her mind.

Lukas bent and grasped her chin. He tilted it up lightly and kissed her gently. "Jenny . . . I did ask you once already. Remember?"

Blushing, Jenny did. And she also remembered the circumstances. She was about to retort, to tell him that a forced answer didn't signify acceptance, but everyone was taking their places at the tables. It was no time to make a scene, Jenny realized.

She smiled uncertainly at her new family every time they beamed at her. The wedding banquet proved extravagant. Her mother had gone all out for the wedding of her only daughter. Course after course of fragrant noodles, chicken, pork, beef, and seafood made the rounds. A battalion of waiters scurried about the garden, refilling glasses.

Jenny's face soon ached from smiling repeatedly at the guests. She toyed with her food, rising obediently every time a toast rang out. The roar of people talking and laughing was deafening. She was probably drinking too much, she realized. She wasn't used to it, and every time she set her glass down, a waiter would appear and refill the narrow glass with champagne.

Her head began to spin. Strains of music sang out from the string quartet hired to play at the wedding, adding to her muddled state. Lukas placed a large knife in her hand, and Jenny looked up at him in alarm. He nudged her. *Of course! The cake!* She recovered and giddily rose to cut the massive wedding cake laid out on a decorated side table. Polite applause greeted her as she walked unsteadily to the cake. Jenny ducked her head and hiccuped secretly. At her side, Lukas looked down at her with concern. ''Are you feeling all right?'' he said.

''Just . . . just a little too much champagne,'' Jenny said. She stared at his white tuxedo, handsomely fitted and impeccably tailored. She remembered the other suit and wondered again if Lukas was involved in something illegal. Perhaps his whole family was, she thought, and burped. Her eyes pounced on his mother's rose-silk suit. Now that she thought about it, she was certain it was a Valentino suit. And his sisters . . . they were expensively turned out as well. If Lukas was involved in something crooked, she realized with growing apprehension, then his whole family was involved.

She weaved around the corner of the table and almost collided with Lukas's father. She stared up at him, but he only smiled and pressed her hand.

''It's a pleasure to welcome you into the family,'' he said. ''We were beginning to think Lukas would never choose a wife.'' His handsome face grew strained. ''A week's notice for the wedding was a bit of a rush,'' he added. ''It was difficult to get away from business.''

Business? ''What kind of business do you do?'' she asked hesitantly. He looked at her wonderingly. His eyes were amber, she saw—the same color as his son's.

''You mean you don't know?'' He sounded amazed. ''And you married my son?''

Jenny nodded numbly.

''Well, isn't he the lucky one? A woman who loves him for himself.'' His face grew thoughtful. ''Yes . . . I think my son would prize that above all else.''

''You never answered my question.'' Jenny knew she sounded rude, but she had to know.

''I'm in shipping, my girl—but I must leave you now,'' he said politely. ''My wife is insisting on selecting dessert for me—do you see her?—she knows I'm not allowed to eat any.'' He patted his stomach and then strode away, an older version of Lukas, but somewhat heavier with middle age.

Shipping! Shocked, Jenny remembered that Lukas had said that smuggling on ships was the goal of Rocky and his friends. Had Lukas been playing a double-edged game to keep his own family's smuggling activities under wraps? Jenny shivered and looked again at Lukas's father. He looked masterful, like a man who was used to leading others. With growing consternation, she realized that Philip Hanh exuded the same aura of power as Lukas.

Have I married into a family of criminals? Her family would never allow such a thing. Or would they? She stared as her father accosted her new father-in-law. The two men talked eagerly as they strolled together to the dessert table. They seemed to be finding much in common.

"There you are." Lukas appeared at her side with a plate generously heaped with cake. "It's delicious. Do you want some?"

"No, I've had enough to eat," Jenny said faintly.

"It's been too much for you all at once, hasn't it?"

You bet, thought Jenny. *I feel like I've been to the moon and back in one day.*

"Maybe I should have waited, but your mother was devastated by her wedding plans being upset. I thought I could please her and surprise you by going along with the original wedding." He grinned wickedly. "With one minor adjustment, of course."

Jenny gave him a strained smile. Lukas put down his plate and suddenly pulled her into his arms. "Jenny," he whispered tenderly. "Aren't you pleased?"

"I . . . wish there could have been more time too," Jenny said. "It's all . . . such a shock. So different from . . . from what I expected."

"I'm getting along famously with your great-grandmother now," Lukas confided. He laughed, and his lips moved to caress Jenny's cheek. "She's already given me a list of names that she thinks would be appropriate for her great-great-grandchildren. I didn't dare tell her that your mother's given me one too."

Jenny had to smile in spite of herself. "My great-grandmother loves children. She's really the one who raised me. She was so good to me when I was little, so patient . . . I can't imagine a better childhood."

Ben approached them, grinning happily. "Congratulations on your wedding day, Jenny." He presented her with a flat package wrapped in white tissue paper. "This is a special present," he confided, his eyes sparkling. Seeing his excitement, Jenny decided to open it right away. Under the tissue she discovered a CD of Ben's first album.

"Oh, Ben," she said. She turned to him, her own eyes sparkling and her worries momentarily forgotten. "I'm so pleased for you."

"It won't be in the stores for months yet. But if anyone deserves it first, it's you. It's because of you that I can still play in a band."

"Thanks," she said gratefully. "I'll play it as soon as I get a chance. I just know everyone's going to love it."

Ben looked at her pale face. "Are you feeling all right? It must have been a big shock to realize you were marrying Lukas." He chuckled. "You should have seen the look on your face. . . . Mother thought you were going to faint.''

''I came close,'' Jenny said dryly.

''Lukas, I'm glad you're the one who ended up marrying my sister. Can I borrow your car sometime? Just kidding,'' he added quickly.

Ben put out his hand, and Lukas shook it enthusiastically.

''Hey, not so rough,'' Ben protested. He held up his fingers and wiggled them. ''These are platinum fingers.'' He laughed. ''And I need them in one piece—I'm going to play a song with the quartet.''

''Ben, you haven't played classical music in years.''

''This one's special,'' her brother said mysteriously and departed.

Lukas moved closer to Jenny, and she looked up at him, wondering how she would manage if he went to prison. She could not deny her longing to have him hold her in his arms forever. But their life could never be a normal one if Lukas belonged to a crime family.

The strumming of a guitar sounded. Jenny's head rose, and she saw Ben standing with an acoustic guitar on the stage. ''This one's dedicated to my sister, the most beautiful bride in Vancouver,'' he told the crowd.

Tears welled in her eyes as she recognized the four opening notes of Ben's song. It was ''Greensleeves,'' a traditional English ballad that she had always loved.

She had often imagined the court lady to whom it was sung—haughty, impeccable, and totally unable to recognize true love when it appeared. She had always wondered if the song had opened the lady's eyes to what she was passing up.

Ben sang the song in a high, eerie tone as he strummed, and Jenny shivered. Would she have to say good-bye to Lukas before their life had even begun? Knowing that she loved him with all of her being, would she be forced to reject him for the honor of her family?

Jenny was quietly thoughtful during the rest of the wedding celebration. Even her mother noticed. "You're acting more like a mature woman already," she complimented after Jenny had danced with her father. "I just know marriage is going to be the thing that finally settles you down."

Jenny looked searchingly at her mother. "Mother?"

"Yes?"

"If for some reason things didn't work out, could I come home again?"

Her mother looked startled. She stared at Jenny's wistful face, and her own features softened. "Don't be afraid to start a new life, Jenny. It's all part of growing up. You won't need to return home—except for visits, of course."

But what if I do? Jenny wanted to say. She thought of her girlhood, neatly put away now among the dolls and other outgrown toys in her bedroom. Jenny found it difficult to picture herself staying there. *No,* she decided suddenly. She was an adult now. If she left Lukas, she would have to manage on her own. Her chin lifted determinedly. After all, she had managed before. And with the success of *Noblesse Oblige* almost certain, Jenny knew she could carve out a life for herself alone.

But being alone no longer held the same enchantment, she realized. She impulsively hugged her mother. *I've discovered I need people,* she thought with consternation. And of them all, her heart cried out, she needed Lukas most.

The rest of the wedding celebration passed in a flash. All too soon, it was time to go. Jenny changed into her going-away outfit—sighing with relief as she escaped the uncomfortable wedding dress—and added a soft bolero jacket. The cream-colored jacket clung to her ribs, showing off the full romantic sweep of the yellow lace dress. She took a last wistful look around her bedroom before leaving. She embraced Miss Lucy and set her back down on the bed. The delicate doll had shared all of her whispered secrets when she was a child.

She stared at the new set of luggage stacked by the closet. Inside the smallest, she knew, a negligee was waiting. It was not something that Lukas would ever have the opportunity to see on her now, Jenny decided. She had made up her mind. She would speak with Lukas once they reached the hotel and finally had a chance to be alone.

She would tell him . . . *tell him that you love him,* her heart cried. No, Jenny thought fiercely. She would tell him that she knew he was involved in criminal things. And then, she thought, her pulse beating raggedly, she would have to tell him she was leaving him before their marriage had even begun.

Downstairs, her family and the gathered guests were quietly expectant, chatting easily among themselves. Jenny paraded down the stairs, her hand sliding familiarly down its smooth, polished rail. The Old One smiled and nodded encouragement.

Congratulatory shouts rang out. Lukas, who had changed out of his tuxedo and into a tan linen suit, reached for her hand when she reached the bottom of the stairs. They ran through the front door. Outside they were pelted with rice—the symbol of fertility the world over—and raced to the silver Ferrari. Laughing, Lucas opened the door for her. He ran around the car to his own door. He warded off the rain of rice with one hand and quickly jumped inside.

"I'm going to have to get the car vacuumed tomorrow," he said, smiling. He shook his head vigorously, and grains of rice flew from his gleaming black hair and onto his shoulders.

Jenny gave him a distracted look. Lukas would have more than rice in his car to worry about once they reached the hotel, she thought.

Chapter Nine

Jenny sat primly on the edge of the enormous bed and tried not to look at the inconspicuous suitcase neatly stacked on top of the other luggage in the corner. Inside was the far from inconspicuous negligee. The sound of the shower running came to her, and she winced, anticipating the scene Lukas would make when she told him she was leaving.

She stared nervously at the twinkling city that stretched out in every direction beneath. They were in the penthouse, and the view window looked out onto the city lights. *They look like a bowl of stars,* Jenny thought, *and the bridge connecting Granville Island looks like a line of fairy lights.* Her eyes followed the fleeing cars heading out to the suburbs of Richmond and Delta.

Going home, she thought distractedly. *They're all going home.* It was not something she would be able to do, Jenny knew. She couldn't bear to return home and confess her marriage a failure before it had even begun. *I can't go back anymore,* she thought suddenly. *I have to go ahead. If I get a cheap apartment until my next book is done, I'll be able to afford something better soon enough. Maybe I can even get my job back at the Jade Paradise,* she thought stoutly.

She lay back on the rose satin quilt and laced her hands over her trim stomach. Flat it would remain, she decided glumly, thinking of babies. She stared up at the cornice moldings of the room and thought of how wonderful everything would be if only Lukas wasn't a criminal.

The honeymoon suite had to be Vancouver's most luxurious. Her mother had booked it months ago. Even then, it had taken some string-pulling by her father to get it for three consecutive nights. Married to Lukas . . . to see his face next to her own each morning when she awoke . . . it would be heaven to stay. The satin quilt felt smooth and inviting against her face, which was still flushed from the effects of the champagne.

But her head was no longer spinning, Jenny thought wryly. She saw things clearly now.

No matter how much she wanted to stay, she

couldn't. How long would her love survive for Lukas once he admitted to being a criminal? She thought of Samantha, the young girl she had met at the club, remembering the coldness in her young eyes. Jenny shuddered. No, she had to face it. Loving Lukas wasn't enough to drive thoughts like that from her mind.

Sarah's breath caught in her throat at the sight of the master bedroom. The dark Tudor paneling had been painted a cheery green. Redecorated in the latest style—she fingered the tapis d'or imported from Belgium and the thick China carpet with its traceries of vines and delicate lilies—not a trace of its former grimness remained. Even the ancient four-poster had been banished. A gilded walnut bedstead with a wreath of carved leaves at the center and an inviting eiderdown quilt trimmed with satin ribbons brightened the room instead.

He had given her so much, she thought fondly. And at last she could give something to him. She smoothed her hands over the cotton nightdress, feeling the ache of her body beneath. They would have many babies, she decided suddenly. I won't stop until the unhappiness has been driven from every room at Greystones, *she vowed.*

A hand reached for hers, and Sarah started, dropping the hairbrush as she felt his form at her back.

"Sarah," he murmured. She arched willingly into him, and his hands moved to unlace the ribbons at her throat.

"No," she said suddenly. She pushed his hands away and smiled at the look of consternation her action had raised on his face. Then she lifted her nightgown and struggled from its voluminous folds. She stood before him, an Eve to his Adam, her wheat-colored hair veiling her like a transient summer cloud. "Do you like me?" she asked shyly.

The bathroom door opened, and Jenny sat up, startled. The shower was still running. Framed in the doorway, Lukas was holding a towel around his middle and staring at her curiously. Her eyes fixed on the smoothly muscled torso in front of her. She wrenched them away with an effort and looked at the floor. Water puddled there, outlining his strong, tanned feet. She swallowed.

"Want to join me?" he asked slyly. "It's a shower for two." Then he noticed her clothes. "How come you're still dressed? I was hoping you'd have something else on by now." He looked quickly at her.

"We . . . have to talk, Lukas."

"So we'll talk—first," he added meaningfully. Lukas padded over to the bed, and Jenny rose hastily to seat herself in a gilded chair. She didn't want that beautiful male body anywhere near her. She could feel herself aching, electrically aware of his presence in the room. The bedroom, which had seemed so large when they had first come in, now felt shrunk to the size of a closet. She shifted uneasily.

"Jenny," he said gently. "What's the problem?" She stiffened on the chair as Lukas drew closer. "Hey—where are you going? I promise I won't get your dress wet." He dropped to his knees beside her. His clean scent filled her with a kind of horror. She struggled as his damp arms rose up to surround her.

"Jenny, it's okay." She felt the warmth of his mouth on her ear. His hands crept to her suit jacket, and Jenny caught at them.

"No," she said furiously. She was fighting not only Lukas, but the insistent part of herself that wanted him to continue, she realized. "I can't stay with you."

Lukas's hands stilled. His amber eyes widened in shock, and he laughed disbelievingly. "We're married," he said, his voice tensing. "You can't still be thinking about that accountant? Are you?" His arms tightened around her, and Jenny cried out, half in anger and half in passion.

Lukas stood up, pulling Jenny upright along with him. "Don't you realize what you do to me?" he whispered. "It's time you found out who you've really married." Jenny wanted to laugh or cry. Instead, she did neither. *Oh, Lukas,* she thought despairingly. *It's no good. I know what I've married.*

''Jenny, I won't touch you, if you ask me to stop.'' Jenny fought to retain control of herself. She opened her mouth to command him to stop, but Lukas took possession of it with his own mouth, with a gentle kiss.

''Oh, Jenny—how I love you,'' he said fervently. He laced his fingers through her hair and drew her head next to his own.

''I . . . I love you,'' Jenny said sorrowfully. He kissed her passionately, and Jenny, unable to stop herself, kissed back furiously. Lukas released her lips and reached out, tenderly moving a wayward strand of hair from her eyes. He was holding her clasped tightly in his arms. Jenny felt secure—protected. Together they were man and woman, yin and yang, two halves joined as one. Her eyes suddenly flew open.

''Lukas! I can't stay with you!'' She struggled away, but Lukas pulled her back, easing them both down onto the bed.

''Jenny, what in the world is wrong?''

''Lukas . . . I can't stay with you. Sooner or later you'll go to prison and . . . I wouldn't be able to bear it. Let me go now,'' she begged, her eyes filling with tears.

He looked at her with growing concern. ''Why would I go to prison?''

Jenny spoke rapidly, afraid that if she stopped, she'd never finish. ''Your father—your family . . . I know you can't help being involved because of your father, but Lukas, it's wrong!''

''What's wrong with shipping?''

''Why . . . everything's wrong with it if you're shipping drugs!'' Jenny looked at him defiantly. To her surprise, he laughed heartily.

Noting her look of hurt amazement, he choked off suddenly. ''Jenny, Jenny . . . whatever made you think my family is involved with drugs?''

''But . . . going undercover . . . you were on the take . . .'' Jenny suddenly wasn't sure what she believed anymore.

''Jenny, when did I ever tell you I was a policeman?''

''You did, when . . .'' Had he? Or had she just assumed that? Jenny frantically searched her memory.

''Jenny, I was working for the police as a special agent. The smugglers were after my father's ships. Somebody who knew our business had to stop it. And it had to be somebody who spoke Cantonese. It took me six months to work my way in, but it was worth every moment of it.''

''Then your father . . . he's not a smuggler?''

''No!'' Lukas exploded. ''Whatever put that idea in your head?''

Not a smuggler! Not a policeman! ''Then who have I married?'' she asked weakly.

"Hanh Shipping." Lukas watched complacently as Jenny's mouth fell open.

Hanh Shipping! It was one of the largest shipping concerns on the West Coast. Her own father's business had dealt with them for years.

"But—"

"I am the only son. Frankly, I was glad to be a policeman for a while. The strain of taking on more and more of the responsibilities for my father was beginning to get to me.

I've got an independent streak, too, Jenny—I've always wanted to see what life was like on the other side of the desk." He chuckled. "Man, did I ever get my wish!"

Jenny nodded. Now *that* she could understand. Suddenly, she began to laugh. All her worry had been for nothing, she realized. She felt wonderful. Except for one thing.

"Lukas . . . how do you feel about writing?"

"I hate paperwork," he said instantly. "I try to do as little of it as possible."

"No—*writing* . . . like book writing."

Lukas cupped her face in his hands. "Jenny, if it makes you happy to write books, that's fine with me," he said gently. He gave her a crooked smile. "I read some of your manuscript."

"What!"

"Why do you think I didn't just trudge away and

let Edward have you? Some of it seemed sort of familiar. . . . I noticed Sir Randolph had amber eyes.'' His own flashed with amusement.

Jenny felt the hot color rise to her cheeks. ''You—you didn't mind?''

''I loved it—I love you, Jenny. Frankly, I was flattered.''

Jenny felt relief wash over her. She didn't have to give up her writing. And she had Lukas too!

''You looked like a proper wife in that red dress,'' Lukas said teasingly. ''Don't you think you should practice taking my shoes off if you're going to be a proper wife?''

Jenny suddenly sprang from the bed and grabbed the towel Lukas had abandoned on the floor. She wrapped it around her body and took three mincing steps toward Lukas. She bowed and then kneeled submissively at his feet. Her head was downcast, but her eyes were secretly dancing.

Lukas sat up, alarmed. ''I was only kidding.''

''So was I.'' She raised her eyes to Lukas, and the distance between them was charged with sudden heat. He swept her off her feet and pulled her to him. Their lips met in a consuming kiss, and Jenny, kissing back as ardently as Lukas, suddenly knew in a full burst of awareness that the Old One was right.

There was no life worth living without honor—and no honor in a life without love.